...And Death Drove On

By Robert Fleming

WILDSIDE PRESS

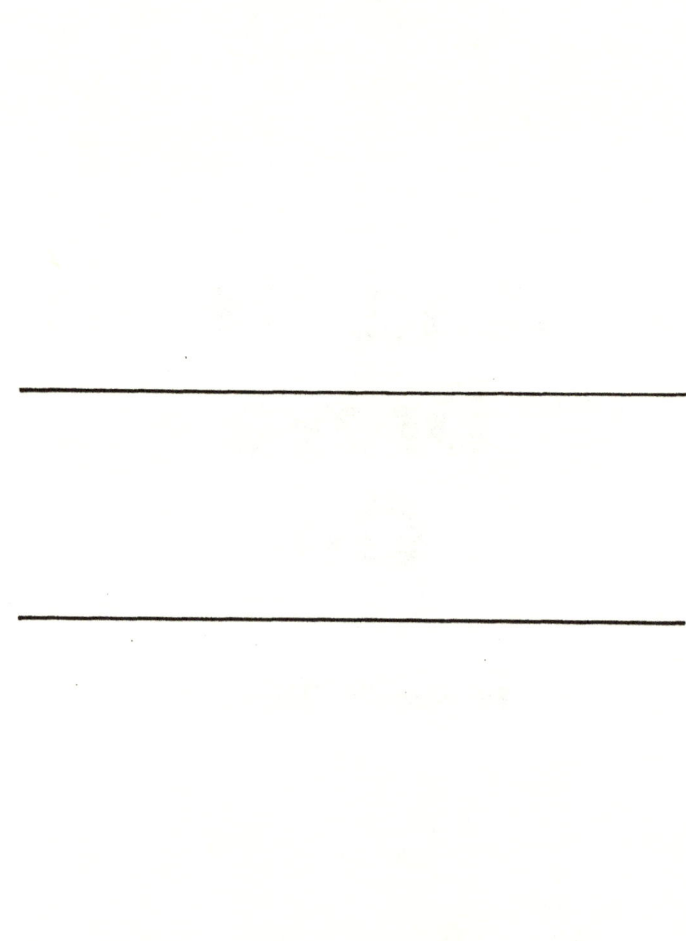

CHAPTER 1

O N THE running-board of a huge truck being loaded at a terminal in downtown Los Angeles, two truck drivers sat and smoked. There was nothing unusual in either of them. One was stocky, tanned and loquacious. There wasn't a shred of inferiority in his manner of facing the world, or dealing with his own conscience.

The second was slender, thin-faced, and a trifle remote. He had a nice face though and a pleasant voice. "What's new?" he was asking the man seated beside him.

The stocky truck driver's eyes slitted. "I got promoted, Ed, since I saw you last. The Trans-Pacific switched me to the night freight division. I go down to Imperial Valley with canned goods, and come back with lettuce, melons or anything that's in season."

Ed Corea puffed moodily on his cigarette. "Ahuh," he grunted.

"For the last three months I've been wanting this run," resumed the stocky man. "I used to haul freight to the docks at Wilmington and San Pedro. Do yet, when it's important. And I was always getting beat up by a tough mob of goons. By God, Ed, I paid dues in two different unions at one time and still got beat up. Figure it out."

Ed said without removing the cigarette from between his lips: "Charley, you talk too much — and too loud. And I've heard you swear. . . ."

"Good God! You've heard me swear? Jeez, Ed, you kidding me?" He spat gustily to the concrete floor.

Ed took a handkerchief from his pocket and rubbed it across a face powdered with dust. "What I started to say was that you lose your temper every time someone asks you to show your union card, or your driver's license, and you start calling men names that smoulder with a low form of oral vituperation. It's no wonder that you get beat up. It's a wonder they don't kill you and take you apart bone by bone."

Charley Kleinhardt seemed inordinately pleased with the other driver's speech. "Every once in a while," he marvelled, unabashed, "you spring something like this oral vituperation on me. You never said, Ed, but did you ever go to college?"

Ed nodded. "What difference does it make? I had to have a job. Driving a truck was the only thing I could find. So I took it. The

3

work isn't too bad — provided I can ever become accustomed to the jar of the cab and the lack of sleep."

"Me," boasted Kleinhardt, "I can stand anything. I've got an India rubber body. But I get to worrying sometimes. Tell me, Ed, what is it you call a man who marries twice without getting a divorce from the number one wife?"

Ed tossed his cigarette away and lighted a second one. He looked tired. "A bigamist, Charley. You should know that one."

"Boy, do I know it. But when a guy adds still a third wife to his other two, what's it add up to?"

"Sheer lunacy. But why this interest in plural wives?"

"Well, it's like this, Ed. I never was one to worry about anything — even my wife. Always I'm away from home, driving here, driving there, and never knowing when I'd leave, or when I'd get back. Home was just a place where I kept a couple neckties and a blue-serge suit. Then a cop wrapped his billy around my head during a disturbance over on the docks.

"When I got normal again and began to look around to see where I'm at, I'm in San Diego, and I've got me an extra wife. I have to laugh, Ed, because I don't remember ever seeing this dame before. Anyways, I splits my pay check and keeps two places going — one in San Diego, and the other in Los Angeles.

"Just when everything is going smooth with my two families, I have an accident. One of the doughnuts on the front wheels blows its top, and the truck and me piles up in a ditch at Capistrano. And Ed, I know you ain't gonna believe me, but it's sure as hell the truth. I lost my memory a second time. So what do you suppose I went and done?"

"You married another woman," sighed Corea.

"You're too damn smart," protested Kleinhardt. "You shouldn't be driving a truck. There's lots easier ways of making money in this town. I ain't driving a truck forever. A guy with brains should only drive his own car. Maybe you know what I'm hinting at, huh?"

"Yeah, sure." Corea's eyelids drooped. "You mean the truck racket — shaking down drivers?"

"Forget it," said Kleinhardt. "I spoke out of turn."

"Listen, Charley," said Corea. "Did you hear anything about the Trans-Pacific truck that crashed into another truck on Route 101 just inside San Diego?"

"I sure did. That truck was in charge of Jake Meyer. Louis Capporiti was riding with him as a helper. They left the truck at the curb and went into a chili joint for something to eat. While they were inside someone stole the cab and trailer. They found it smashed three blocks away and a load of iron castings missing. I happened to be in San Diego when the truck disappeared. The company never found out where the castings went, or who stole them."

"You know," said Corea, confidentially, "there was something funny about the crash and the theft of those castings. They weren't castings at all. Did you know that, Charley?"

Kleinhardt's lips twitched slightly. "They were billed as castings. That's all I know."

"Maybe they were. A lot of unusual freight is run at night. But there was only one thing in that truck trailer — a motor. It was one of the best motors of its type that ever came out of the Glendale shops. I was intended for a newly-designed fighting plane of the United States Navy. Didn't know that, did you?"

Kleinhardt examined a broken finger nail. "Nope, Ed, I didn't know it. How come you found it out?"

Corea shrugged. "What difference does it make?"

"I just wondered," said Kleinhardt, rising to his feet. "Well, I got to get going. Be seeing you soon, Ed."

He slouched away through ranks of trucks and trailers, walked to some steps leading to the loading platform, followed a narrow space between rows of cardboard cartons, and stopped at a point where a box had been nailed to the wall. Inside this box was a telephone.

For several moments he regarded it intently, reached for it, changed his mind, then started to chew reflectively on his lower lip.

CHAPTER 2

AT THE end of a hall on the seventh floor of a downtown business building was a door with a frosted-glass panel. Printed on the glass were the words: SIMON CROLE, SPECIAL INVESTIGATOR.

In the agency's reception room as one entered this door, sat the private detective's secretary, Etta, cherubic, bland and efficient. Two doors opened from this reception room. One led to a tiny room usually occupied by Crole's only operator, one Matt Ridley. The second door led to Simon Crole's more spacious office where he dealt with honest and dishonest clients who came to him for the solution of their problems.

Two men sat in chairs facing the bland secretary. To a young woman she had just assigned to a chair between the two men Etta was saying, "Please be seated. Mr. Crole will be here in five minutes." She smiled urbanely on all three visitors and made notes on the time each had entered the office.

Half an hour later the hall door opened. Into the reception room padded a big man who walked with the lightness of a cat. Myriad wrinkles slanted fanwise from the corners of his eyes. An old scar, that twisted his lips slightly out of alignment when he smiled, gave his round, priestly face an expression of perpetual surprise.

There was an aura of sacerdotal benignancy about Simon Crole that masked his petty dishonesties; a streak of Puritanism in his character that shielded him from larger ones. A trencherman of no mean ability, he loved the pleasures of the table — and the bottled cheer that comes from grain and grape.

Gravely he accepted the slip of paper his secretary handed him. And as gravely he read the names of his callers and their business with him. The men looked doubtful. Still, there was a possibility that gold might be separated from the amalgam of their several problems. And his agency needed it — or its equivalent.

"Please be seated," he nodded to the first client to enter his private office. "Your name, I believe, is Gordon West. You have a problem although you haven't stated it yet. Understand, Mr. West, that I reserve the right to accept or reject, as the case may be, the problem you present. Is that clearly understood?"

Gordon West shrugged and sat down. The chair creaked beneath his weight for he was as big a man as Crole. Cold blue eyes stared around the room as though he was taking mental notes of the exits. His jam was square, hard. Before speaking he took a panatela from his pocket, lighted it and continued to look around.

West puffed leisurely. "There's a man in this city that's causing me trouble. I want him removed."

"That's somewhat of a blunt order, West."

"If you're thinking I want him destroyed, you're both right and wrong. I'd prefer the courts to handle him when I'm through with the preliminaries."

"Just what have you on your mind?"

"I want dictaphones installed in this man's office. I want his telephone wires tapped. I want access to all his office records."

"There's a law with teeth in it covering that sort of thing, West.

Police and government agents can tap telephone wires and install dictaphones with impunity. But a private detective with my standing can't assume the risk. My license to operate is worth more to me in the long run than any fee you might pay me. That's the way it is. I can't accept your case. As a matter of fact, I don't want it."

West examined the growing ash on his cigar. His eyes had become sullen. "Just why are private detectives like you in business? What are you supposed to do besides mess around with divorce cases? You have your price. Name it."

"I'm in business to make money, West. But as I remarked at the beginning of the interview, I reserve the right to pick and choose. What you have suggested is, frankly, out of my line. It has an *odeur* of disagreeableness. It reeks."

"With what?"

"With grief, West."

"Then you won't take the case?"

"Bluntly, no! Consider the interview closed. Good day."

"Okay, Crole." West got to his feet. Banked fires glowed momentarily in his blue eyes. Turning abruptly, he stalked from the office.

Placid indifference flowed over Simon Crole's priestly face as he watched Gordon West leave. The second client came into the room.

"Your name," Crole began, "is Enoch Morgan, and you've come to see about collecting certain monies due you. I'm sorry, Morgan, but this is not a collection agency. My secretary notes on her memorandum that you are a gambler. The natural inference is that these are gambling debts. Right?"

Gambler Morgan nodded. "But I have their I.O.U.'s. Don't they suggest anything to you?"

The private detective spread his hands palms up on the desk. "Only sheer futility. Again I must apologize. Collecting debts from men who have lost at gambling always gave me a headache. I want none of it."

Morgan shrugged and got to his feet. "Thanks anyway," he said. "Can't blame me for trying."

"Not in the least. Here's a tip. Try the Risnor-Kelley agency on Broadway at Fifth. Tell them I sent you."

"Thanks again," said Morgan. "I have a hunch they'll play cards."

"So have I, or I wouldn't have dealt you the hand."

She came in regally, did the last of the three callers — a woman,

and a strikingly beautiful one. Her black hair hung straight down
to her shoulders, and the ends were curled into a single ringlet. She
wore a tailored suit of dark broadcloth and a flattish hat of the same
material. The faintest suggestion of a smile hovered around her
carmined lips.

Simon Crole stood up when she came towards his desk. "How do
you do, Miss Edmunds," he bowed with exaggerated courtesy.

Esther Manning, a former operator in Simon Crole's agency, and
now a very excellent woman lawyer, dropped negligently into a
leather upholstered chair near the desk. "You were so intent," she
told him, "staging a show to impress men who might possibly be
future clients, that you never even looked in my direction when you
came in. That's all right, too. What I was interested in was not you,
but Mr. Gordon West. Please tell me what he wanted."

"Gordon West," he replied, "approached me with a proposition I
did not care to handle. What he desired of me was the installation
of dictaphones in someone's office, and the tapping of telephone
wires. But why — what is your interest in the gentleman?"

"A woman's intuition — something I can't explain. I met the
Wests at a party in Beverly Hills. Something in the way they acted
focused my attention on them. I made discreet inquiries, and discovered that all was not well in the West household. But that's all I
did discover."

"Ummm!" grunted the private detective. "And Mrs. West. What
sort of a woman is she?"

"Charming and extremely good looking. She has all the virtues of
an angelic wife, but none of the vices."

"The allegorical significance escapes me. Am I to gather the impression that Mrs. West has retained you as her attorney in the
eventuality that such services might later prove useful to her?"

"No. Charlotte West hasn't asked me to work for her yet. But I
hope she will. That was my reason for coming to see you. It was
entirely accidental that Gordon West entered the building just as I
was thinking about entering it myself. I followed him a few minutes
afterward. Since I was but one of a group of nearly fifty at the
Beverly Hills party, he did not recognize me. So I came in and sat
down right next to him."

"And discovered that your woman's intuition has played a scurvey
trick on you. You deserve a good dinner tonight."

"Thanks. Are you asking me where I'd like to go?"

"No," he said. "I've got other plans. Tonight, at eight o'clock, I am sitting down to a banquet at the *Commodore* as guest of an old friend of mine from the New York City Police, Inspector Ira Fletcher."

"Oh, well," shrugged Esther, rising. "I might have known."

"The Inspector and I were on the Homicide Squad together for years. He wouldn't hear of my not being present when he delivers the speech I practically wrote for him."

Esther smiled brightly. "Have a good time, Simon."

"I'll have a good time eating, but I expect to sink into a state of morbidity before the evening's over."

" 'Bye," she called back from the doorway.

" 'Bye," he sighed.

CHAPTER 3

THE NATIONAL Convention of Police Officers, judges, ballistic experts and dabblers in crime opened auspiciously around fine linen, silver and sparkling glass. Chief of Police O'Connor was present. So was District Attorney Minifie. So, likewise, was Captain Jorgens who bore the brunt of fighting on the skirmish line of robberies, riots and homicides.

County Sheriff Hernandez, an amiable and keen executive was also present with a number of his smartest aides. Present also were members of the bar, and a host of Los Angeles police officers from the lowest to the highest rank on the force. Decidedly, this was no place for a criminal. He'd have as much chance as a liver pill among a gathering of hypochondriacs.

The subject of inks is a fascinating one. Doctor Bier of Milwaukee was going into it thoroughly following the demitasse. Said the Doctor in part: "Inks may be classed in three divisions: nutgall, aniline and logwood. Since these writing fluids have special uses and properties easily recognizable by the use of a tintometer, acid reactions and black light photography, they assume a place in criminology quite as important as finger prints.

Simon Crole nudged Inspector Ira Fletcher. "The pompano," he whispered. "It was nothing more than butterfish. You noticed the deception of course?"

Inspector Fletcher yanked a black cigar from between his teeth. "What the hell's pompano?" he whispered.

"The fish course, Ira. Did you not know that you were eating butterfish disguised as pompano?"

"I never eat fish."

Simon Crole relaxed, took out paper and tobacco, and rolled a consoling cigarette. The discovery of the fraud practiced on him by the menu mildly disturbed him.

Doctor Bier finally finished his discourse on ink and turned over the floor to a compatriot.

By nine o'clock fingerprints were out of the way, and Inspector Ira Fletcher was well into his lecture on questioning suspects, possible witnesses, and the use of the third degree.

Sheriff Hernandez spoke glibly and well on the two-way radio. Chief of Police O'Connor explained the value of cooperation between city, state and county law enforcement officers. Then Police Captain Jorgens got to his feet. He was a ponderous, dark man with eyes that smouldered with the seriousness of his profession, a man who chewed cigars incessantly, who eyed all men with frank suspicion, and whose life was dedicated to his great passion — law and order.

"Gentlemen," he began, and as he spoke the room was completely silent. "Only a few minutes ago, word was brought to me concerning the outcome of the Grand Jury's deliberation on possible indictments against racketeers and gamblers. It is imperative that we continue to restrain men of criminal tendencies from preying on our citizens. For this we are well-equipped. But gentlemen, what are we to do when these same criminal tendencies are present in our own organization?" Simon Crole gave the speaker a startled glance. "Perhaps I am entirely out of order in bringing the subject up. If so, I am sorry, but nonetheless determined to drive out the human termites undermining, not only my own department, but others as well."

He nodded somewhat grimly towards an officer smoking a very fine cigar — a heavily-built lieutenant of detectives. "Lieutenant Berchtold, you are not suspected, at least by me, of undercover activities. But you undoubtedly know more than you care to admit concerning the renegades within the departments. I have my own source of information for this statement. Chief O'Connor, will you support me in this?"

"Sorry, Captain Jorgens. But I cannot. This is a police officers' convention, not a criminal hearing."

A bleak smile froze the Police Captain's face. "And you, Mr. District Attorney?"

"The police department is beyond my jurisdiction in the present crisis," stated District Attorney Minifie, smoothly. "I refuse to be drawn into something that is definitely out of place at this time."

Jorgens chewed on the unlighted cigar and stared morosely at the faces of two judges who might have spoken in his favor, but who didn't. He looked from the judges to the faces of attorneys and out-of-town police officers. If he had any friends in the gathering, they certainly weren't breaking their ankles jumping to their feet.

The eyes of the Police Captain finally alighted on the round, priestly face of the private detective next to Inspector Fletcher. He scowled, and sat down.

"Anyone else having anything to say at this time?" asked the presiding officer.

Simon Crole sighed, puffed out his lips and got to his feet. "Mr. Speaker, and gentlemen. As a private detective and a guest of Inspector Ira Fletcher from New York, I rise to make a protest. It seems to me, and probably to a great many others who find themselves in a position where they can't speak what is on their minds, that Captain Jorgens is well within his rights in bringing up the subject of graft and corruption within the police department.

"If you have two good eggs, one bad egg, and break them in a dish together, does that make them all good? Unfortunately, it does not. It makes them all bad. Contamination fastens itself to the good ones and pollutes them. I hope the analogy is clear.

"If Lieutenant Berchtold has anything to say for himself, and isn't afraid to talk — he should be made to talk. By publicly disciplining Captain Jorgens, you have made a stupid mistake — one you may later regret. I thank you."

Pandemonium broke loose. The District Attorney and two police officers jumped to their feet.

"There is a time and place for all things," thundered the District Attorney. "And a convention banquet is not the place for the public airing of. . . ."

"It's a lousy play to the gallery," shouted Berchtold, "and Captain Jorgens knows it. . . ."

"Gentlemen, gentlemen!" The presiding officer's water glass, used in place of a gavel, hit the table twice, then splintered in his fingers.

Inspector Fletcher turned untroubled eyes on the private detective at his side. "You started some fireworks, Simon."

"Roman candles," said Crole, "for a Roman holiday. Captain

Jorgens and I aren't what you might call friends, but we have a working arrangement arrived at through trial and error whereby my agency collects on criminal cases, and his office takes the credit of arrest and conviction. Berchtold has Jorgen's job in mind, and he's the most ruthless police officer I have ever encountered."

Berchtold by this time had the floor. He looked over the convention delegates with sullen contempt. "I've got nothing to say, now, or any other time. . . ."

"But *I* have," broke in a voice that up to this minute had not been heard. A thick-chested man with lines of dissipation on a hardened face lurched from his chair at the table. "I've got plenty to talk about — enough to rip the city's police department wide open."

"Sit down," said Berchtold, ominously. "Who are *you*, Scanlon, but a second-rate private dick. You were fired from the San Diego police force. You furnished mobs of tough strike-breakers for the shippers during the last Pacific coast tie-up. And now you're running a private detective agency. Bilge! The city ought to run human scavangers like you and Simon Crole out of town on a rail. Your places are cesspools breeding crime."

Crole whispered to Inspector Fletcher: "Evidently the Lieutenant doesn't like me."

Inspector Fletcher lighted a fresh cigar. "Ummm!" he grunted.

In the background, against the wall, moved a photographer from the *Clarion*. In one hand he carried a tripod to which the camera box was fastened. In the other he held an electric lamp with a wooden handle at its base. Trailing behind him was a long, rubber-covered extension cord that kept getting snarled on table legs.

"Cesspools of crime, eh?" repeated Scanlon. A snarl turned the corners of his lips downward. "And bilge. Okay, Berchtold. Listen to this. I've been investigating, and I know what I'm talking about. I have positive proof in my possession that certain citizens in this town have been regularly shaken down by police officers under the protection, and orders of. . . ."

The explosion of the gun sounded far away. It was a sound that was difficult to place. It may have come from the outside. It may have come from the inside of the huge banquet room. The eyes of the convention delegates turned questioningly as each sought confirmation from those next to them. No one became excited. There seemed to be no reason for even the mildest kind of alarm.

Berchtold sat down. His face was inscrutable.

Captain Jorgens pawed at the wire bristles of his mustache.

District Attorney Minifie impatiently moved his wine glass from one spot to another on the white cloth. Inspector Fletcher became concerned with the ash at the end of his cigar. And Simon Crole searched his pocket for a watch. It was three minutes of ten.

The reaction to the ominous sound was slow in starting. These veteran representatives of police organizations were accustomed to the sound of exploding guns. Their minds had not yet bridged the gap between cause and effect for they had not expected anything of a homicidal nature.

Eugene Scanlon was still erect beside his chair. One hand clutched the back of it. The hand was trembling. His other hand was groping upward in short, halting movements. The coloring on his face had become faulty — as though bathed with a palish, green light. It accentuated the lines of dissipation etched around eyes and mouth.

For several fatal seconds he stood gripping the chair in pained, stunned surprise. His lips twitched as if moving them had already passed beyond his control. And when they eventually came apart, his mouth assumed a corpse-like leer. "Payoff," he croaked. His eyes became glassy. The lips twitched a second time. From them issued a twisted jargon of syllables that sounded faintly like: "And I ain't fraid of Ed."

His knees buckled then, and he fell grotesquely across the banquet table, staining the white linen with a crimson stream that gushed from a small bullet hole in his chest. He was dead before anyone could reach him.

CHAPTER 4

EARLY WEDNESDAY morning two squad cars of police officers left Headquarters. One sirened out to the living quarters of the late Eugene Scanlon.

In the deceased man's apartment the officers found an electric refrigerator stacked with liquor, a closet filled with a miscellaneous assortment of clothes, but no records, no papers, and no clues were discovered as to why anyone should want him murdered.

The second car broke all traffic regulations getting down to Scanlon's office on Spring Street. When they finally got the door unlocked and had surged inside, they discovered that someone had been there before them. Whatever records Scanlon possessed had been carried away. There was nothing left but some odd pieces of furniture, a creaking typewriter, and a stack of unpaid bills.

The murder of Eugene Scanlon in the banquet room of the *Commodore* might have happened in any large city — Cleveland, Birmingham, or New Orleans. Homicide is as ancient as the rock that slew Abel. It was unfortunate, however, that the crime took place before the eyes of over a hundred police representatives who were trained to prevent and solve such crimes. Yet no one had prevented the crime. And no one seemed to know who had committed it, or from which direction the bullet had come.

Although Los Angeles was accustomed to weathering shock, both from earthquakes and criminal vandalism, this shock jarred the city fathers and the Police Commissioners out of their inertia.

Lieutenant Berchtold was questioned. He could tell the Commissioners nothing. And that was exactly what he told them. They transferred him to the Central Division Jail.

Inspector Jameson of the Rackets Detail was called to the front. So far as he knew, the force was honest to the last man. Him they cashiered to the Traffic Division. They questioned Captain Jorgens for a number of hours. And the hard-boiled Captain's ignorance of why Scanlon should be murdered was as abysmal as that of his two fellow officers.

The President of the Police Commissioners, an honest and unimaginative business man, looked Captain Jorgens squarely in the eyes and gave him the ultimatum: "Find Scanlon's killer in three days — or resign."

The ubiquitous *Clarion* pounced upon the ultimatum like a hired man reaching for the plate of fried chicken. In the vernacular of the street, this sort of thing was right up the newspaper's alley. In an eight-column spread, covering the whole front page, appeared the dire headline: DEATH RUNS AMUCK AT POLICE CONVENTION: Then in smaller type ran the sub-heading: "Police Captain Jorgens ordered to find Scanlon's killer in three days, or resign."

There was no reason why Simon Crole should have read these items when they appeared in the press. True, he had a certain interest in the crime since he was present in the banquet room when Eugene Scanlon had come face to face with death.

And yet, contrarily enough, he read everything printed — not half-heartedly, but with a great deal of concentration. Lips pursed, he studied the interior photographs of the banquet room taken after the convention had adjourned.

Two of the camera shots were exceptionally clear as to detail. One showed the body of the murdered man sprawled across the table in a puddle of liquid from overturned water and wine glasses.

The second picture, taken from another point, probably from a spot near the main entrance to the room, not only revealed the body, but a considerable portion of the room. And as Simon Crole studied the most minute details of the photograph, he became aware of something he hadn't noticed the previous evening. The room had been gaudily decorated with streamers of crepe paper, but since the *Commodore* was an old hotel, there were a number of round, steel supports for the banquet room's ceiling. Fastened to these supports were strips of crepe paper that held sprigs of fern. He counted the decorated posts. There were six of them visible in the picture.

Yet only one of them claimed his interest. He wondered, idly, if the police had noticed that one post. Should he call Police Headquarters and notify Captain Jorgens of what he had discovered? He decided against such a move. Still, his interest, being what it was, could not be denied some outlet.

He took down the receiver of his desk phone. "Precious," he said, "Get me a line to Inspector Ira Fletcher. He's staying at the *Manhattan*."

After a few moments Inspector Fletcher's voice rumbled from the receiver. "Yeah?"

"Ira?" said Crole. "Simon speaking. What part of the banquet room would you say the shot came from that killed Scanlon?"

"Immediately in back of where I was sitting. Say, are you crowding in on something that the police will zealously regard as their own particular problem? If you are, I'd advise you to lay off. They won't take kindly to outside investigators."

Simon Crole shrugged this advice aside. "Call it professional interest, my friend. I was curious regarding an acoustical problem. Would you take an oath that the sound of the gun was behind where you sat?"

"Damn right. I've got good ears."

"Remarkable. Similarly, if I were on the stand, and the question was put to me, I would say, with equal honesty and belief, that the gun was fired from a spot to the right from where we sat. And my hearing is just as keen as yours."

"Then why the devil are you asking me what *I* think? I've talked with four of your city officers, good men too, and none could agree on this one point you have raised."

"Unerringly, my friend," sighed Crole, "I have blundered onto a moot, but important angle in the shooting. Here's another one. Which way was Gene Scanlon facing when the bullet struck him?"

There was a silence at the other end of the line. Finally Inspector Fletcher said: "That's a poser, Simon. I don't know. And that's peculiar. But it's the truth."

"Don't feel badly. I admit I don't know either. And this point of agreement is also important. We're both fairly observing. Yet we can't agree on the direction of sound. A remarkable organ the ear, Ira. In man and other mammals it consists of an auricle, or external ear, for collecting sounds; a tympanum, or middle ear, for transmitting these sounds; and a labyrinth, called internal ear, for delivering them to the end-organs of the auditory nerve."

"You kidding me, Simon?"

"No. I'm simply explaining something I thought you ought to know."

"And fogging the issue. I say that the sound of the gun came from in back of where I was seated. And I'll stick to that statement. By God, I ought to know what I hear, and where the sound comes from."

"That's what *you* think, Ira. I'm prepared to take an oath that the sound of that gun came from my right. And we'd both be wrong."

"How do you know?"

"I'm merely stating a truth that has not yet been verified, but which, nevertheless, can be proven in time. Now let's get back to Scanlon. We're both in agreement that we don't recall the direction he was facing when the bullet struck him."

"Yeah. Go on."

"Which would indicate quite plainly, my friend of long standing, that our attention was not on Scanlon — but on someone or something else."

"Maybe you're right at that. But I don't recall anything."

"How about the photographer?"

"That's it. I was watching him untangle his electric cord extension."

"So was I. Now. Was there a wind blowing last night?"

"Huh! What's that got to do with . . .?"

"Was there, or wasn't there a wind blowing."

"No!" roared the Inspector. "There was no wind . . . Ha!" he chortled, "unless you are a stickler for truth and want to include that wind-bag who was lecturing on moulage procedure. Bah! Moulage. Sissy stuff. Give me a suspect, and to hell with his footprints. I'll sweat the truth out of him . . ."

"I'm talking about nature, not human beings."

"Consider me squelched. But what the hell! You've got something on your mind, Simon. And I know from past association with you that you'll keep it hidden. Then, if you've made a mistake, you won't have to admit to a wrong theory."

"Don't be that way, Ira. I haven't any theory — not yet. I'm trying to puzzle out a detail I discovered in a flashlight picture in the *Clarion*. Study this picture yourself, and see if you don't uncover the same thing I did. Remember, you and I are going to have dinner together tonight. Don't forget it. Come down to the office anytime after five."

He hung up, moistened his lips, and looked appraisingly at a colored lithograph of The Darktown Fire Brigade hanging awry on the wall.

Presently he got out a tobacco sack, papers, and rolled a cigarette. After lighting it his fingers dropped idly to the desk top and began to drum out Flatfoot Floozie.

He heard the elevator door clang shut followed by the click of heels, obviously plated with metal, along the tiled corridor. The heels skidded to a stop at the door leading to the hall.

A client, he thought, brightening.

Etta's honeyed voice purred through the partly opened door to the reception room. "How do you do. Is there something I can do for you, officer?"

Simon Crole knew his secretary's bland method of attack. When she was overly-polite, and the honey in her voice was stickily sweet, it meant that the enemy had crashed the portal, and there was little she could do but warn him over the interoffice phone.

"That's right, sister," said the man who had just entered. "And you can tell Crole I'm from the Police Department — Lieutenant Berchtold. He'll know who I am."

"Send him in," he told her quietly over the phone.

Through the door connecting the two rooms strode Lieutenant Berchtold, his jaw set at an arrogant angle. "Where's Gordon West?" he snapped.

"Sit down, Lieutenant," said the private detective, masking with a hypocritical smile the antagonism he felt.

Berchtold flung his body into a chair and allowed his eyes to drift around the office. "You must be making money fast, Crole?"

Simon Crole refused the bait. "You asked about West. I don't know where he is. Should I?"

"Why not? He's supposed to be a client of yours. I was informed that he had you in mind for a certain, under-cover deal against Gene Scanlon. He was also observed going in and coming out of this building yesterday afternoon."

"He came here," said Crole. "He saw me. We talked several minutes together. Then he left. I haven't seen him since, nor do I expect to. Nor did I accept him as a client."

Berchtold shrugged. "We'll drop West for now, and get down to something personal. Why did you get up before the delegates last night and tell them I ought to be forced to talk?"

"Civic pride, Lieutenant," said Crole, rubbing his chin with the heel of his hand. "I had a notion, after hearing what Captain Jorgens insinuated at that time, that you were keeping a number of things to yourself. Whether you were doing this for your own advancement, or to discredit your superior, Captain Jorgens, I do not know. But I still insist, Berchtold, that if I were the head of the Police Commission, I'd have made you talk, and talk plenty."

"What makes you think I have anything to say?"

Crole shrugged. "Only the statement of your superior. He remarked that you were not suspected, but that you did know more than you cared to admit concerning the renegades within the department. Now don't get me wrong, Berchtold. I don't care one way or the other. Your quarrel is not with me, but with your superiors in the police department — and the dead Gene Scanlon. Fortunately, for a number of people, Scanlon's mouth is forever closed. But even dead men have an annoying habit of talking — in some form or other — long after they've passed on."

Berchtold got up from the chair. His eyes were hard. He spoke slowly and with emphasis. "If you're smart, Crole, you'll keep your fingers out of something that doesn't concern you. There is trouble enough in the police department without private dicks like you and others trying to tell us what to do. Write that down on your memorandum pad so that you won't forget."

Simon Crole still had the hypocritical smile on his face. "I never write things down, Berchtold. I carry everything in my head."

He was still smiling as he watched the police officer pass through the doors to the corridor. For several moments he sat in the chair, his eyes roving aimlessly around the room.

Matt Ridley, Crole's only operator, came lounging out of the small room adjoining the inner office. He was a slender man with wide shoulders, a perpetual grin, and a vast awareness of his own ability.

He wasn't by nature sufficiently endowed with gray matter to ever make a first-class private detective. His mind moved always in a single, narrow track from which it could not be swerved. Complications upset him. Crole could never be certain what Ridley would do under stress. Yet Matt Ridley was a hard worker, afraid of nothing, and loyal beyond any form of bribe.

"If you should ask me, boss, I'd say offhand that Berchtold is trying to cover-up."

Crole blinked at his operator. "Cover up what?"

Ridley said airily: "Somebody's mistake."

"Do you think he had a part in Scanlon's death?"

"I wouldn't know offhand. But if you want me to, I'll find out where he stands on the case. All I need is some wood to make a door out of, then opportunity will come along and start kicking it down. I'm so good at private investigations that . . ."

"Let's dispense with the panegyrics, Matt. If you can get anything on Lieutenant Berchtold, get it. Right away."

Ridley pushed a battered felt hat to the back of his head. "You mean that, boss?"

Crole nodded.

"Okay. I'll talk to some of the cops who work under him. They oughta know, seems like. Boy, I'll find out soon enough. How about some expense money. I'll have to buy some drinks."

"Get it from Etta on your way out."

CHAPTER 5

DRIVING THE MACK tractor with a twelve-ton load in the trailer was no job for a weakling. Ed Corea drove with care, keeping well to the right on U. S. Highway, Alternate 101 on the trip south to San Diego. He shifted gears at the right time on the grade leading into Costa Hermo, came to a crawl at an intersection stop sign, dropped into creeper gear and churned across the intersection. By the time he reached the town's outer limits his machine was rolling fast.

A few miles out of Costa Hermo, on a side road well screened from Highway 101 by two rows of Eucalyptus trees, stood a black sedan. There was nothing distinctive about the car. It was but one of thousands of its particular make. Even its driver was inconspicuous. He may have been a stevedore, a salesman, a rancher, a truckdriver, or a gunman — though there was nothing suggestive in his appearance that indicated any one of these. He wore a darkish suit that was large for his stocky frame. There was a suggestion of the outdoor man in his tanned, leathery face. And a veiled, icy glitter occasionally appeared in his eyes.

Beside the sedan was a white motorcycle with a windbreak in front of the handlebars. Astride its saddle, with booted feet resting on the hard-packed adobe soil, was an officer in uniform. He did not look happy. His right foot kept tapping the ground as if he were impatient with things.

"Getting jittery?" asked the man in the sedan.

"Who wouldn't," growled the officer on the motorcycle.

"You should have wised yourself to certain obligations when you were having a tough time passing your Civil Service examinations . . ."

"Skip it," said the officer.

"Maybe you don't like the system?"

"It isn't a question of liking anything. Forget it, will you? I'm doing what I'm told. Doesn't that satisfy you?"

"Hell, Merkle. I'm not your boss. I'm just one of the mob — a liquidator, the Big Shot calls me. You know what a liquidator is? You don't know. I don't, either. It's one of those new words for a guy who pours out liquor. If you and me knew words like liquidator, we'd be big shots, too. Ain't that right, Merkle?"

"You talk too much," said Officer Merkle. "Now listen. I don't know you. I don't want to. Somebody above me tells me to work with you today and follow your instructions. I don't. . . ."

"Sure, sure. Now don't get sore. Ah!" His eyes were on Highway 101 where it curved out of Costa Hermo.

As the tractor and trailer rolled over the rim of the distant hill he raised a pair of Zeiss binoculars and trained them on the truck license plate near the front bumpers. The letters and figures stood out clearly. He compared them with a license number he had scrawled on a dirty piece of cardboard.

"XC-4577," he read. "Driver, Ed Corea. Hmmm!" Momentarily, the icy glitter returned to his eyes. He'd have to handle this business smooth so that Merkle would not suspect it had all been arranged in advance. There must be no kickback.

Aloud he said to the officer on the motorcycle. "It's a Trans-Pacific truck with a fairly new driver at the wheel. His name is Ed Corea. Only been with the company a few weeks. His trailer lights were put out of order at the Terminal before he left. So that's one violation. You can think up the rest yourself."

"Has he got any cash with him?"

"He was paid with a check this morning, and got it changed to bills at the office just before starting out."

"What's he good for?" asked the officer.

"Twenty-five bucks easy."

Officer Merkle nodded, kicked down on the starter, and drove his machine down the dirt road towards U. S. Highway 101.

The thin face of Ed Corea was expressionless as he braked to a stop on the wide shoulder along the edge of the concrete highway at the motorcycle officer's curt order: "Pull over."

"What's the idea, officer?" he asked, turning off the switch.

Merkle's mouth twisted into something that was intended for a questioning smile. "So you don't know, eh? New driver, aren't you?"

"I've made two trips to San Diego. This is my third."

"Hmmm! I'm going to check your running lights. Step on your brake pedal. Just as I thought. Lights out of order. That's the usual thing with you careless drivers. All right. Turn on your trailer lights. Also out of order. What kind of a driver are you anyways? No lights in the rear at all. That's bad, driver, plenty bad — especially the stop lights."

"I can't understand what happened to the lights, officer. They were all right last night."

"Yeah? You drivers all have the same story. I get sick of hearing it. The lights are out of commission now, and they've probably been that way for some time. When's the last time this crate was inspected?"

"Three days ago." Ed Corea climbed down and examined the lights that were out of order. Two of them looked as if they had been deliberately smashed.

"All right," continued Officer Merkle. "Let me look at your operator's license, bills of lading, and your hourly report card."

Ed produced the proper cards and papers.

Merkle examined them casually. "Okay," he said.

"Can I drive on?" asked Corea.

"No. Not yet. Not until I get the ticket made out."

"Oh !"

"What do you mean, oh? I've got you cold for three violations. Lights out of order. Speeding. And passing an intersection light without coming to a full stop. Been drinking?"

"Not a drop."

"You don't act drunk, and that's a fact. But you've been driving as if you were. I've been trailing you for seven miles. I think I ought to take you back to Costa Hermo for a sobriety test. How'd you like that?"

"I wouldn't mind it at all, officer, if I wasn't in a hurry. I've got to deliver this load to a warehouse in San Diego and get back to Los Angeles before dark. Can't the charge be fixed?"

"What makes you think the charge can be fixed?"

Ed Corea shrugged. "You can't blame me for trying. As a general rule, most things can be fixed."

"Tell you what I'll do," said Officer Merkle, confidentially. "I'm not hard-boiled like some of the other cops. At the same time I have to keep a careful check on you careless drivers and protect myself."

"Ahuh !" nodded Ed.

"These violations will cost you twenty-five dollars if we settle this infraction of traffic regulations out of court. Take it to a Justice court and it will cost you fifty, maybe, as well as the loss of time away from your job when the case comes up."

"Twenty-five won't break me, officer."

"I don't want to break you, driver. My motto is live and let live. See? Here's how it works. There's nothing to keep you from turning me in — depends on how you feel about paying *me* the fine instead of a judge. If you make a report and turn me in, I'll probably lose my job for accepting what is termed as a bribe. But don't forget that you are the one who bribes me, and you'll be held equally guilty, and the violation will stand against you."

Ed Corea took a thin roll of bills from his pocket and counted out two tens and a five. "Do I get a receipt?"

Merkle regarded him coldly. "What do *you* think?"

"I just wondered, and I thought I'd ask."

"Better get going," advised Officer Merkle. "You said you were in a hurry to reach San Diego."

"That's what I said, officer. But I don't believe it matters much whether I get there today or tomorrow. How long has this sort of a racket been going on over this highway?"

Merkle's lips curled. "Asking wise questions, eh? I've got a damn good notion to sock . . ."

Ed Corea slid an automatic from beneath his armpit. "You aren't going to sock anybody. Keep that in mind. I've got an excellent preventer of that sort of thing to back up my protests. Raise your hands, officer. That's fine. I should hate to smear your nice uniform, but I'm afraid I'd have to if you chose to get nasty. Now. Get those steel cuffs from the back of your belt and snap them around your wrists. You're riding in the cab with me. And we're heading for the nearest sheriff's office."

A frozen grin spread over his thin face as Officer Merkle fumbled for the handcuffs. He heard the smooth whine of tires on the concrete behind them. Out of the corner of his eyes he saw a black sedan.

"You're going to regret this," growled Merkle.

Corea shifted his gun so that it couldn't be seen by the driver of the black sedan. He wasn't in any mood for explanations to passing motorists.

Merkle raised his voice until it was almost a shout. "Better put that gun away, driver, before you shoot somebody."

Corea was watching officer Merkle through narrowed eyes, but his mind was centered on the car somewhere behind him. It wasn't going on past. It was stopping. He turned his body slightly. It was difficult to watch both car driver and police officer at the same time.

The driver of the sedan stepped to the ground and came over to where Corea stood with gun leveled at Merkle. "Is that nice," he said, "to point a gun at an officer of the law?"

"Huh!" grunted Corea, instant recognition lighting his face. "You?"

"Yeah. It's me. I got a swell job now, travelling for a wholesale candy firm. This is part of my territory. Well, it's the first time I've ever seen anything like this. It's a grand idea holding a gun on a cop. I like your nerve, Ed. Are you going to kill him?"

"I'm thinking about it," said Corea, grimly.

"Don't let me stop you." He reached casually into his pocket. "Have a candy bar, Ed?" His hand came out of the pocket like an uncoiling whiplash. In it was a lump — not candy, but a deadly Police Positive. He fired twice with merciless precision.

The bullets struck Ed Corea like powerful sledge hammers, jarring him from his stance in front of Officer Merkle. Weakness flowed down his legs. He collapsed, coughing and clutching at twin holes in his chest.

He knew as he fell that he had lost to a man he had not remotely figured as an enemy. And the knowledge was tragically bitter. He hoped, with the last flitting thought that crossed his mind, that others wouldn't make the same mistake that he had. Then Ed Corea stopped breathing.

Officer Merkle began to swear. "I hate this rough stuff. It's going to be hard to get away with. I think I understand now what you meant when you called yourself a liquidator. But you're nothing but a goddam gunman. This driver's liable to die on us."

"Suppose he does? Maybe that's what I was sent out here for — to see that he does die."

"You'll hang if the department pins a killing on you."

The sedan driver did not seem disturbed. Cars kept passing on the highway, but the black sedan partly shielded the body of Ed Corea lying close to his truck. And the presence of the white motorcycle kept motorists from being too inquisitive.

"Listen, Merkle," he said, "Ed Corea knew too much, was too damn interested in certain things that happened. He wasn't a real truck driver any more than you are. There won't be any trouble over this business if you listen to me. First we'll trade guns. They're both Police Positives. Then you're to tell your superiors that this driver threatened you with an automatic. See? You had to shoot in self-defense. Justifiable homicide is what I was told to tell you."

Merkle knelt down and examined Corea's body. "He's dead."

"You just finding it out?"

Straightening to his feet Merkle said: "I'm not taking the rap for you or anyone else. That's out. I'm willing to play along . . ."

"Now, Merkle. Use your head. You've got more brains than I have. You sure have. And I guess you forgot the wife, your two kids, your new car, and house that is almost paid for. I guess you've forgotten where the money has been coming from. I'm not asking for a cut on the twenty-five you collected. That's all yours, Merkle. Am I right?"

"Yeah," shrugged the officer. "I guess you're right."

They traded guns, but it was obvious that Officer Merkle didn't like the arrangement. The other man didn't seem to care. He slid his stocky body behind the wheel of the sedan. "Don't worry," he called out the window. "Self-defense. It'll be a cinch. You'll be taken care of by the right people. You sure will."

Officer Merkle again swore under his breath and began to chew on his finger nails. His eyes were shot with cunning and suspicion as he watched the sedan wheel around and head back toward Los Angeles. Then they swerved to the ground and followed it to the spot where the body of the dead man lay close to the front wheels of the tractor.

Whatever he did must be done swiftly. There must be no mistakes. His story must hang together and be absolutely flawless. He had signaled the truck to a stop. Made out traffic violations. Corea had protested, got mean and had drawn a gun and fired it point blank.

The explanation of the shooting seemed a little weak. It needed bolstering. He bent down close to the lifeless figure on the ground. His own cap! He removed the uniform cap from his head and tossed it to the ground. Up and down the highway he looked. Luck was still on his side. No cars in sight.

The cold automatic was still nestling in the stiffening fingers of the dead man. Merkle wrapped his own hand around those fingers and brought pressure to bear on the trigger finger. The gun held by two hands jumped as it exploded. So did Merkle's visored cap as a .38 calibre bullet whipped through the gabardine cloth.

The officer retrieved the cap and placed it on his head. It was all clear in his mind now. Corea had shot first. The bullet hole through the cap furnished undisputable proof. It pleased him that he had thought all this out in detail. And suddenly he knew that he was master of a bad situation.

Striding to the highway, he flagged the first passing car to a stop and said to its driver: "Stop at the Police Station at Costa Hermo. Tell the officer in charge to send one of his men down here at once. There's been an accident. Also have an ambulance sent down."

He lit a cigarette after the car had driven away, took three puffs and ground it out under his heel. Tiny muscles in his stomach began to draw into a knot. In spite of the first feeing of mastery, he was beginning to feel that everything was not quite perfect. He kept his eyes averted from the body beside the truck. He looked nowhere but at the concrete road leading to Costa Hermo.

"You're goddam right," he kept muttering to himself. "They'll take care of me. They've got to. You're goddam right."

CHAPTER 6

MISS URSULA GAULT, secretary for the deceased private detective, Eugene Scanlon, sat primly behind the ravaged desk of her former lord of conceits and deceits. A tall, spare woman of uncertain age was Miss Gault; a member of three religious cults, and a horse for work. She had a sly sense of humor and a wen on her left cheek.

Her hair was parted in an uncompromisingly straight line down the middle of her skull. She deplored cosmetics. And drank spiritous liquors only after sustained religious doubts.

No man but Scanlon had ever looked twice at Ursula Gault. Her bleak eyes created a frosty barrier that concealed a warm sentimentality of which she was at times ashamed and afraid.

Only the dissipated Eugene Scanlon had ever peered beyond the frosty windows of those bleak eyes and seen warmness, human kindliness and loyalty. So he had grabbed her, growled at her, flattered her, swore at her, put on an act whenever she threatened to leave his office, raised her salary — and in secret, admired her ability, if not her gaunt body and plain face.

She now held the fort that was hers by right of possession. Mr. Scanlon was gone. "Foully done away with," she wrote to Martha, an invalid sister, "by a dastardly and unprincipled person."

She knew as well as anyone that there was no lucrative reason why she should remain longer in the citadel of intrigue without the cunning rogue — Mr. Scanlon. There were, no longer, any confidential reports to type; no filing; no threatening letters to write; no more lies to repeat. She was without a job. And there was nothing for her to look forward to but the dreary prospect of loneliness and the terrors of job-hunting.

Her gaunt face brightened momentarily as she reviewed in her mind the row she had had with the policemen when she found them in the citadel that was the office — her office. And her sturdy heart picked up extra beats when she remembered how efficiently she had berated the inquiring reporters.

In the voluminous and daily letter to Martha, she referred to the police as boisterous, libidinous, hard-headed apostles of law and disorder. And the reporters," she had scolded, "were foul-mouthed, lecherous slingers of innuendos that stopped just short of libel."

Her bleak eyes travelled upward to an aged clock on the wall. Three o'clock. Two hours yet before closing time. She shut her jaw aggressively, picked up a pencil and began to concentrate on the names of people who owed Mr. Scanlon fees for services rendered.

Vandalism. Work of small boy. Hardly worth prosecuting. Settled out of court. Fee reduced to $10.00.

"Harvey Glencannon. Chief Mate of coast freighter, *Rosa-Rosa*. Infidelity. . . ."

Miss Gault had found something tangible to grasp. Something to take her spinster mind from the rape of her citadel. She didn't need the account book stolen during the night. She had all the facts and figures stored away in the neat cubby holes of her mind. And she was going to re-create it all — everything. Feverishly she applied herself to the self-imposed task.

Sometime later, a mail carrier pushed a letter through the mail slot in the hall door, and it slithered to the floor.

Miss Gault raised her bleak eyes, then her spare body, walked to the spot where the letter lay on the floor, and picked it up.

The stray letter, written in Eugene Scanlon's own atrocious handwriting, was addressed to Mr. Edward Corea, 749-B South Hill Street, Los Angeles, California. Scrawled across its face in pencil were the words: "Moved away. Left no forwarding address."

A dead man's written words had come back to the point from which they were dispatched, and the dead man would never know they had come back. Even the man to whom these words of instruction were addressed would never know, for he was beyond needing instructions anymore. He was with Eugene Scanlon. And Scanlon was dead.

Miss Gault filed the unopened letter between an old-fashioned cotton undervest and her tailored, pique blouse. There was no hurry about reading the letter now. She was going to have plenty of time in the long hours ahead — when the last day of the rent was used up. After that. . . .

Primly she pursed her spinster lips and wrote what she afterwards erased. "Dear God. What am I going to do now? Martha is so helpless. And there is no one but me. How am I going to take care of her when — when I can no longer stay here?"

Simon Crole sat at his desk tinkering with a cigarette lighter that seldom worked. He looked like a benevolent Buddha intrigued with some earthly problem. He smiled slightly as the Police Captain came into the private office, and a look of surprise seemed to flow over his priestly face.

"How are you, Captain Jorgens," he said. "Know anything about fixing these trick lighters?"

Jorgens dropped heavily into a chair facing the private detective. "You're looking at a man, Simon, who is on the verge of insanity. By tonight I'll be frothing at the mouth or chewing the leather walls of a padded cell."

"I think," said Crole, "that the spring is busted. There is supposed, according to the inventor's original plan, to be considerable pressure exerted on the piece of metal beneath this wheel. Observe, Captain, that when I rotate the wheel with the ball of my thumb . . ."

"From the padded cell," Jorgens resumed, "it is only a step to complete imbecility."

"However," Crole shrugged, "the gadget never worked to my satisfaction. Either the flint wore out, the wick gummed up, or the fluid evaporated. Never, to the best of my knowledge, did all three of these necessary appurtenances function at one and the same time."

Jorgens's eyes squinched almost shut. "Then throw the thing out the window! I tell you I'm losing my mind. I'm going crazy, berserk. The system's going to steam-roller me . . ."

"Rubbish!" shrugged Crole. He laid the lighter reverently away, reached into the bottom drawer of his desk, and removed therefrom the bottle of golden Bourbon. "While you're collecting your scattered wits so that you can speak intelligently, I'll see if this Bourbon has, by any chance, started to deteriorate. You're on duty, I believe."

"Of course I'm on duty. I'm always on duty."

"Then I won't offer you a drink."

"I ought to kill you," husked the Captain.

Simon Crole filled to the brim two wax-paper cups, pushed one of them across his desk, smiled and said grimly: "You're among friends, Captain, believe it or not. Drink. Then talk. Three days is a short time when your job hangs in the balance. I don't think much of you, and you undoubtedly think less of me. Let's forget bygones and be friends."

"No. I'm not forgetting anything. Someday I am going to have the exquisite pleasure of slapping you in a cell and exposing your . . ."

"Gene Scanlon had the same notion about some members of the Police Department. He was all ready to expose them, but he never got quite to it. Why did you send Berchtold here to make inquiries about Gordon West?"

"If Berchtold came here, he did it of his own accord. Who is Gordon West?"

"He's the head of a large trucking concern."

"I'm not interested in West, Simon. I want the murderer of Gene Scanlon. That's all I *do* want. Did the Lieutenant think that West had something on Scanlon?"

"He didn't say."

"Why'd you bring in his name?"

"To find out what its all about. There's a hostile attitude within the Police Department. It was quite apparent last night. Which explains why I stood up for you, Captain, when I knew you were wrong. My admiration for your bullheaded determination went up several notches. Right now my agency is in the doldrums. Do you want my help on this case. Answer yes or no."

Jorgens became wary. "We don't need any outside help."

"Damn it, Captain," said Simon Crole testily, "Why'd you come here then?"

"To get a fresh grip on my sanity."

"Nonsense. You came here to get rid of some of your meanness and to see if I had any theories. As a matter of fact I have several. I'd keep these theories to myself if I had any use for them." From his desk drawer he removed a picture he had taken from the *Clarion*. Before showing it to the police officer he said: "Do you know definitely from which direction, and from where the murder weapon was discharged?"

Jorgens shook his head. "No. Everybody I questioned who heard it had different ideas. It's impossible to find two persons who agree on the direction of the sound."

Crole nodded. "Even Inspector Fletcher and I are in disagreement and we sat beside each other. Know why? The accoustics of that banquet room tosses any sound around so that it seems to come from everywhere at the same moment. Now take a good look at this picture and see if there is anything suggestive in its detail."

Captain Jorgens regarded the picture sadly for nearly five minutes. "No. I don't see a thing. I thought for a moment the face of the murderer was going to show. But I guess that's out."

"Not much chance," said Crole, drily. "The picture was taken after everybody had left. Now look," pointing with his thumb. "Do you observe the position of this particular streamer of crepe paper? Oh, you do? And you're aware that it is a part of a rosette fastened to the ceiling between two posts. Whoever decorated the room knew his business. Observe also that the streamer has been torn away from its anchorage in the rosette."

He sighed and continued. "It was certainly not torn away by the wind for none was blowing last night. And it was too high for anybody to brush against accidentally. Yet, it's been ripped away from the rosette so that there are two ends of the streamer showing. And that small, dark spot, right there, Captain, is a small hole — a bullet hole."

"Damn!" breathed Captain Jorgens. "You've got eyes like a lynx."

"You can see what I'm pointing out then?"

"I'm not blind. Of course I can see it."

"Then my eyes are no sharper than yours. It amazes me, Captain, that you ever rose so high in the police bureau."

"I fought my way up, step by step. And I'm still fighting every day and hour to hold on to what I've earned through hard work. But that's my business. If you've got any more ideas about me in that head of yours, I'd thank you to keep them to yourself."

"Peevishness is common to us all, Captain. I stand corrected, but the amazement persists. However, we digress. Now, suppose we draw a straight line from the spot where Scanlon stood when the bullet struck him, and extend it through the crepe paper to its logical end. What is immediately apparent?"

Jorgens mentally drew the line. "The shot came from a narrow window high up on the west wall."

"That's correct. There are three of those windows along the west wall, and they open onto an alley at the street level. The banquet room is below the level of the street. At night the alley would be fairly dark with little or no traffic. The spot was ideal for the purpose. Whoever was at the window must have been reasonably certain that Scanlon was going to talk out of turn, and was prepared to stop him if he started to say too much. Is the window open?"

"It is, according to the picture," admitted Jorgens, grudgingly.

"Listen, Captain. I didn't take the picture. It was snapped by a newspaper photographer. And if the window seems to be open, you can take the camera's record that the window was open. And whoever fired the lethal weapon was outside that window — not inside. Automatically then, every police officer in the room is eliminated as a suspect. That's something to keep in mind."

"I appreciate the fact that you're enamoured by the sound of your own voice, Simon. So keep on talking. Maybe you'll be of help to me after all."

"Didn't my tip to gather in the records from Scanlon's office help you any?"

"Unfortunately, no. Someone got there ahead of my men."

"That's worse than unfortunate. It's a miserable break for the Police Department. I think I'll visit the office myself."

"Not much use. There wasn't as much as a scrap of paper in the files when my men arrived. Nothing. And Scanlon's secretary — a shrew of a female with a tongue like an adder — gave them holy hell when she got there and found them pawing in filing cabinets. If she had been a man, they would have smacked her down."

"Your boys lack the right touch where women are concerned. Why didn't they use their brains and treat her with respect?"

"They were in a hurry, and were looking for evidence."

"You just told me that the office had been thoroughly cleaned of everything — even to the last scrap of paper in the files. What was there to look for?"

"I don't know. Whatever it was, my men never found it. Their report of the search covered three sheets of paper. An excellent report, by the way, describing the movements of three men from the moment they left my office until the hour and minute they returned. But it meant nothing — absolutely nothing."

"How many men do you have close to you in the department that you can trust?"

"Plenty. But there are just as many that I cannot and dare not trust, men who are capable, men who know their jobs. A number of these officers obtained their jobs through political connections. Some got in by purchasing the answers to Civil Service questions. Don't ask me how, and why there haven't been prosecutions. A number of people would like to know that — including myself.

"And it's logical enough that the loyalty of these officers is going to be showered on the person who helped them into the service. If I start an investigation, and it centers around an individual of importance, the investigation will bog down. Records will strangely disappear. Witnesses will fade into the blue. And, though I threaten officers till my larynx wears out, I still won't get the right kind of cooperation. And my superiors will say to me: 'Captain Jorgens, either break this case, or resign.' On the surface the problem seems simple. But underneath it boils with intrigue, suspicion and distrust. Everybody is afraid of everybody else."

Simon Crole sighed heavily. "Captain," he stated, "I don't want a thing to do with this case. It reeks. Solve it yourself or resign. In a moment of weak sentimentality, I offered to help you. The offer was a mistake. I withdraw it. I should have known better. Take the picture of the banquet room. I don't want it around."

"Give me another drink," ordered Jorgens, "and shut up! Who's asking you to help me? Nobody. Who's even hinted that I needed help? Same answer as before. Ah! Thanks, Simon. There's nothing I admire about you except your choice of whiskey."

"You've admired it for years, Captain, bottle by bottle. But I've never seen you bringing any in to replace what you've poured down your throat."

Captain Jorgens got rather lumberingly to his feet, walked to a window and stood for a time glaring down at the crowded sidewalks. Presently he muttered something unintelligible and returned to Crole's desk.

"Listen. I'm talking to you now as man to man, and not as a police officer to someone outside the force. The department needs help from the outside. I doubt if anyone but you can solve this crime. Will you do it?"

"Anyone would think I was infallible," said Crole. "But I can make just as many mistakes as you — or anyone else. Do I get any assistance from the police?"

Captain Jorgens shook his grizzled head. "No. That's the unsual part of what I'm asking you to do. I want you to work independently from my office. Personally, I'll do whatever I can to assist you. But it won't be much."

"That's all right, too. At least we won't be tramping on each other in a mad search for clues. Well, Captain. Three days is a short time. And the first day is nearly over. I'd better get busy and find this man known as Ed. Maybe there will be some money in it for me somewhere."

"Ed?" The eyes of the police officer narrowed. "Who the hell is Ed?"

"I don't know any more than you do. Have you forgotten Gene Scanlon's last words just before he pitched forward to the top of the table?" He smiled benevolently. "They sounded like this to me: 'Payoff. An' I ain't 'fraid of Ed.' Remember?"

"Yeah," murmured Jorgens. "I remember."

"The solution to murder is contained in that cryptic utterance. I have the feeling, Captain, that Scanlon, who was dying, mouthed these words to such an extent that they suggested something he did not mean to say."

"You mean we heard wrong?"

"We heard what he said. But not what he meant. The words don't belong together in sequence. There is something odd in the way they're strung together. They rasp against my ears disagreeably in a lingual discord of sound."

"Imagination, Simon," rumbled the Captain, getting to his feet. "I heard what he said. And it sounded rational to me. Better try another angle."

"I'll undoubtedly try several. Meantime, how will I contact you in case of an emergency?"

"Phone my office. For identification use the number eleven. Don't give your real name, and don't use any phone that can be traced."

Crole yawned. "Okay, Captain."

"And keep that dumb operator of yours — Matt Ridley — out of the investigation. He'll only mess things up."

"That's why I keep him on my payroll, Captain. He is a positive genius for uncovering odd pieces of information that are priceless. Curiously enough, he is never aware of it at the time. I couldn't run the agency without him."

Captain Jorgens grunted, walked from the office, glared at Etta's bland smile when he reached the reception room, and slammed the corridor door behind him.

"What a sweet disposition that man has," remarked Etta, loud enough for Crole to hear her.

The private detective got up and padded out to the front office. "Did you take down in shorthand everything that was said between us?"

She nodded prettily. "Everything except swear words."

"Tear the pages from your notebook. Destroy them. Dynamite couldn't be worse. My life wouldn't be worth a counterfeit penny if, the man responsible for Gene Scanlon's death knew that Jorgens had given me a free hand in the investigation."

His voice trailed away. The knob of the corridor door was turning slowly. The door opened. A young, clear-eyed patrolman stood in the opening. "Is Captain Jorgens here?" he asked.

"God forbid," said Etta, piously. "There's trouble enough in this office without him being around to make our life miserable."

"Okay, sister. Gosh, you're a swell looking dame. I'll be seeing you sometime." He closed the door, and they both heard him walk down the hall.

"Now what could that cop have wanted?" asked Etta.

"Evidently," said Crole, quietly, "the Captain is being watched."

CHAPTER 7

A T FIVE minutes to four Simon Crole walked down a hall in a Spring street business building and came to a stop before a door bearing the name and profession of Eugene Scanlon. Even as he slowed to a stop he heard a woman's voice from behind the door panel.

"No. I'm sorry. But I refuse to leave the city, and nobody can make me."

The eyebrows of the private detective lifted. He hadn't expected any melodrama, yet here it was sifting through a doorway and filling his ears. Evidently someone was trying to tame the shrew by sending her places she did not wish to go. It was too late now to turn back. They must have heard him coming down the hall. He hadn't been quiet. He knocked twice and pushed open the door.

Behind a desk sat Miss Ursula Gault, competent, neat and certainly not in distress. Facing her, but with his back to Crole, sat a man wearing a new, gray suit. The man twisted around in his chair as Crole came in. He had a square face, heavy jowls, and a shock of iron-gray hair. His lips were tightly closed. Suspicion warped his eyes.

"H'are you, Scanlon," beamed Crole, extending his hand. "My name's Jackson. From Cedar Rapids, by jeepers, and I'm here to see you on business of a personal nature."

The suspicion went out of the eyes of the man in the gray suit. He shrugged his shoulders and started to explain that he was not Eugene Scanlon.

Miss Gault cut in: "I'm sorry, but you've made a mistake."

"Eh? Mistake? I saw the name on the door. Eugene Scanlon. And I can read pretty good. Heard Scanlon was darned good in some ways. By God, I'll need a good man to find that wife of mine. Big woman, blonder than a faded cornstalk. Talkinest woman in seven counties. By Jeez, either she divorces me, or I divorce her. Don't make no special difference so long as we get shut of one another."

"I'm sorry, sir," said Miss Gault, "but Mr. Scanlon met with an unfortunate accident. He died last night."

"Well now," breathed Crole, suddenly deflated. "That's right unfortunate. And me expecting to get his help doing something or other about my wife who's the talkinest woman . . ."

"Excuse me," broke in the man with the gray suit, rising to his feet. "I'll drop in tomorrow sometime, Miss Gault. By that time I think you will have changed your mind."

"It's barely possible," said Miss Gault.

"Soon as you finish your business with this man, Miss, I'll tell you some more about my wife. Damnest woman in seven counties."

The hall door slammed behind the man in the gray suit. Crole's sleepy eyes studied the gaunt, plain-faced woman who was no longer Eugene Scanlon's secretary. So this was the shrew with the tongue like an adder? Her eyes, he could see, were sharp. She wore cuffs made of rolled sheets of paper to protect the sleeves of a tailored blouse. For some reason, this pleased the private detective.

"Well," she told him. "There's no sense in your remaining. There is nothing *I* can do for you."

"That's too bad," said Crole in an altered voice — his own. He opened the door, looked up and down the hall, saw that it was empty, and very softly closed the door again. A benign smile bathed his priestly face. "There is more you can do for me than you think. Who was the man who just left?"

Ursula Gault sensed a flank attack by a new enemy. And she was never known to shrink from battle. "Get out," she told him. "I've told you and your filthy tribe everything there is to tell. Now there's nothing more. Get out before I put you out."

"Softly, madam, I mean you no harm."

"And you needn't madam me. I know your kind — sneaking contemptible scavengers that prey on the carcasses of humans in distress. Jackals in men's clothing, buzzards in shirts and neckties, termites gnawing at . . ."

"I've been called everything but a termite, madam," said Crole, his eyes twinkling. "Frankly, you couldn't mean that?"

Miss Gault's eyes blazed. "Out !" she ordered.

"More and more," he told her, making no move to leave, "I admire your spirit. You're not a beautiful woman. No doubt Gene has told you this many times. But you do have your points. And courage is not lacking."

Ursula Gault called up fresh reserves of invective for a final assault on this benevolent enemy.

"You are not a shrew," he observed, dropping into the chair lately vacated by the man in the gray suit. "You're simply a woman who has been pushed too far. The symptoms are readily observable. You're not only angry at the man who just left, but you're equally angry at me for no reason at all. Your attitude is unjust, unfair and unladylike."

"Will you stop talking and get out?" Her voice dripped acid.

"Presently. Will you listen to me?"

"Why should I?"

His priestly face registered a questioning calm. "A fair question. I'm not from the Police Department. I'm not a reporter. I'm a private detective."

She laughed with fine scorn. "Holmes of Baker street, perhaps."

A gusty sigh pushed the private detective's lips apart. "No, madam. My name is Simon Crole."

"Oh!" She watched him closely, hiding her eyes behind slightly lowered lids. After a moment she said, "What . . . do . . . you . . . want?" She enunciated each word clearly and separately.

"I want," said Crole, and intend to find, the murderer of your late employer — Gene Scanlon."

"What was he to you?"

"A name merely, but also a member of my own profession."

"I've heard Mr. Scanlon speak of you. He referred to you as a suborner, a procurer, a crook and a glutton."

"Mouthings, my dear. All of the horrible things Mr. Scanlon might have called me can scarcely be true. My faults are legion, the devil knows. And as such they are my personal concern. I have not come here to argue the vices of Simon Crole. I have come here to argue vices of other men."

From his pocket he removed a wallet. "It is reasonable to infer, madam, that you are no longer on a salary basis. Am I correct?"

Miss Gault suspected a trick, but the sight of Crole's wallet whetted her curiosity. "I am," she thought guiltily, "about to be offered a bribe."

"It was my intention," said Crole, "to add you to my payroll temporarily — provided, of course, that you would accept a slight honorarium of one hundred dollars."

"Where is the catch in all this?" asked Ursula Gault.

"My dear," said Crole, rising, "there is none. I believe I stated quite plainly that I wanted and intended to find the murderer of your late employer. It will make it easier if you work with me. If you refuse, I can't force you, nor do I intend to. You have a choice. Submit to the threats of the man who just left this office, or work with me. You can have your pay in advance if you want it."

She did not hesitate. "I'll work with you. And you need no longer call me madam. My name is Miss Ursula Gault."

From his wallet Simon Creole removed a sheaf of bills. "I'm paying you in advance, Miss Gault. Which should indicate that I trust you completely."

"Thank you," she said.

He placed the retainer in her hands. "You will report at my office at six o'clock this evening. We'll have dinner together with some friends of mine. Oh, you won't need an escort. . . ."

"Experience taught me that long ago, Mr. Crole." There was a faint trace of wistfulness in her voice.

"You are not only a wise person," he told her, taking her cold hand in both of his, "but a modest one as well. Wear the nicest things you have, Miss Ursula. We'll make this party an occasion."

He bowed, put on his hat and left her.

Ursula Gault collapsed after he had gone. With trembling fingers she took from the desk drawer the last page of a letter she had been writing to her invalid sister, Martha. With an air of determination she dipped a pen into an ink bottle and wrote:

"P.S. I live in a world of utter confusion and cross currents. Perhaps my prayers have become jumbled, for the fine hand of the Devil seems to have created a macabre situation in which I seem to be the exact center. A most charming, and glib-tongue rogue has entered my life. . . ."

In the throes of composition, her eyes lost their coldness and became ecstatic. A warm flush suffused her face, softening its gaunt lines. She finished the postscript, sealed the envelope, and almost ran down the stairs to the street.

Simon Crole was in a hurry. He had gone to his apartment to change into evening clothes. From this point he called his former operator, Esther Manning, on the telephone.

"My dear," he told her. "You're dining with me this evening in company with Inspector Fletcher and a wilted, but sturdy flower by the name of Miss Ursula Gault. I . . . listen, my legal friend, this is no time to quibble. I want you to be with *us*. It concerns the death of Gene Scanlon. . . . Uh-huh. Of course it's none of my affair. But I have a hunch, my dear, that somewhere in the background of all this there is a nice fee to be collected. Who's going to pay the fee? Really, I can't answer that one. The telephone is no instrument over which to discuss monetary details. At a quarter of seven Inspector Fletcher will call for you in a taxi. Be nice to him." He closed the connection.

Close to the Trans-Pacific Terminal, set back in a sprawling driveway that was a convenience to big trucks, was the chili and hamburger stand of José Gracios.

Charley Kleinhardt had just entered the building. Throwing his stocky body on a stool with both elbows on the counter, he ordered coffee and pie. José's wife, buxom and beaming, poured coffee from a Silex bowl into a mug, cut a wedge of raisin pie and placed them on the oilcloth-covered counter.

After giving her a dime Kleinhardt buried his face in the coffee mug. Deftly, then, he divided the wedge of pie into six segments, eyed them longingly for a moment, then gulped them down.

While he was pawing with his fork at the last crumbs on the plate a red truck belonging to the Lightning Express curved into the driveway. Its driver got out of the cab swearing at the steady downpour of rain. He came in stomping and slapping his cold hands against the sides of his wet slicker.

"Hyah !" said Kleinhardt.

"Hyah !" repeated the driver. "Oh, it's you, Charley. Geez, what a day. And me on my way to El Centro. Hell, ain't you working? You're all dressed up like you was going to a wedding."

"My day off," said Kleinhardt.

"You're lucky," grunted the newcomer. "Service please. Java and pie, *Senora.*"

The buxom wife of José Gracios cut another wedge from the raisin pie and slid it onto a plate. After the truck driver had eaten his pie, he said to Charley Kleinhardt: "Hear about the shooting down the road today?"

"No," said Kleinhardt. "I've been sleeping all day. Who's been doing the shooting?"

"I got my info from Nick Pargas. He picked it up from Jeff Rider. And Jeff heard about it in the court of the Justice of the Peace in Costa Hermo where he was having a session with the judge for getting caught speeding through town."

"I haven't heard anything about the shooting," acknowledged Kleinhardt, peering into his mug to see if he had overlooked any drop of Gracios coffee.

"It's going to be a long, tough trip down to El Centro if this rain keeps on, Charley. My tires are as smooth as baloney skin, and the lousy outfit I work for won't do a thing about it. I think I'll try and land a job with the Inter-State outfit. Then I can go places like Arizona and Texas. Man, there's a sweet run. All new country."

Discovering there was no more coffee left, Charley Kleinhardt pushed the mug away and said: "Did Jeff Rider say who did the killing down the road?"

"How'd you know a guy was killed? I haven't told you yet what Jeff told me."

"Go ahead. Tell me."

"Well, it was like this. The man who was shot drove a tractor and trailer for the same outfit as you work for — the Trans-Pacific. A motorcycle cop flagged him down. Ed got mad, hauled out a gun and put a neat hole through the cop's derby. So the cop hauled out his own gun and went to work on the driver. What else could he do?"

"Don't ask me," shrugged Kleinhardt, fumbling for a cigarette.

"Well, figure it out, stupid. I don't blame the cop at all."

"You called the driver by the name of Ed. What's his last name?"

"Corea. His name was Ed Corea."

Kleinhardt stared hard at the design in the oilcloth covering the counter. "I've met the guy. Kinda slim he was. Smart, too. He didn't belong on a truck, that guy didn't."

The Lightning Express driver finished his coffee and set the mug down with a thump. "That's the name all right. Ed Corea. He shot the cop's hat clean off. An inch or so lower would have been just too bad for the cop."

"Tough," said Kleinhardt. "I knew this guy, Corea. And he didn't seem like a man who goes around carrying a gun."

"Yeah!" chortled Lightning Express, sliding off the stool. "Them's the kind of guys you gotta watch. Them smart fellows think too much. It get's them after a while, and they go haywire all in a lump."

Kleinhardt did not take his eyes from the figured oilcloth. "A man never knows," he said, morosely. "Like I said. He wasn't the kind of a man who goes around carrying a gun. He was a quiet guy." The expression seemed to please him. "He sure was a quiet guy."

CHAPTER 8

WHEN SIMON CROLE arrived at his office a few minutes before six, he found his secretary smiling with the complacency of a cat who had just finished a dish of thick cream. She had on her hat and was doing something to her eyelashes.

"Going somewheres?" he asked.

"Stepping out," she said. "With a police officer, believe it or not."

"Not the one," he blinked, "who was . . . ?"

"The same. He came in and made a call after you left. I was nice to him. He fell for me hard. Tonight we go places, him and me."

"Sounds like your grammer has gone on ahead of you. Is there anything else I ought to be told?"

"He's a rookie patrolman with ambition. His name is Terrance Doyle. And he's a fast worker."

"That's fine. What else?"

"Else? How could there be anything else. We haven't said more than a dozen words to each other."

"Perhaps in those dozen words you discovered which side of the fence he is on. You must have learned that much."

"Not a word. We talked about dance orchestras, swing, shag. . . ."

"This office is deteriorating," he complained. "Anybody call?"

"A memo concerning Mr. Matt Ridley is on your desk."

"Ummm! If you will abandon temporarily, precious, whatever it is you're doing to your eyebrows and render a straightforward report of what's taken place here since I left, the report would be gratefully appreciated."

"Your sarcasm is out of place. I've already attended to my duties as your secretary. Your memorandum pad is black with notes, telephone numbers, and things you must do before curfew rings tonight."

He explored his freshly-shaven jowls with the back of his hand. "I intended," he mused, "to arrange for a private room at the *Lambeth Inn* on Hollywood Boulevard earlier in the day. By any chance do you recall my asking you to take care of the reservation. . . .?"

"I recall nothing of the sort. You may have had the intention, but you never expressed it."

"Do it then. Now. Call the place and ask for Louis. Explain to Louis that you overlooked making the reservation earlier. Tell him the private room is for Simon Crole and three friends. Tell him we'll be there by seven o'clock."

He left her then and padded into his private office, sat down behind his desk and regarded with a curious lack of interest the notes on his memorandum pad.

Matt Ridley had been in the office during his absence. His report was brief and somewhat startling. It read: 'Hold everything. I'm on the track of something big colossal. It's a good thing you put me into this investigation. I'm doing swell. My expense account will be quite a jolt to the agency. I got some extra cash from Etta, the little miser. Anyone would think it was her money I was spending. Matt.'

He dropped Ridley's note in the wastebasket with a quiet sigh, and pored over two telephone numbers he was supposed to dial. Grunting, he consulted the city directory for a clue. He thought of several people and dully checked their names against the numbers. They didn't check. He shrugged and laid that memorandum aside. Calling strange numbers at this late hour was not in the least intriguing. He did not call them.

There was also a penciled memorandum having to do with telephone service which he laid aside unread. He wasn't interested in the telephone company. Then his eyes brightened as the door to the reception room opened.

Inspector Fletcher, glum and huge, bulked in the opening, "Let's eat," said the Inspector.

"Restrain yourself, Ira," Simon admonished. "First, you're taking a cab and making a crosstown journey to the home of Esther Manning. Then you're to go to the *Lambeth Inn* — Esther knows the place — and wait for me there. I'll be along directly to join you. About seven I hope. Meanwhile I'm waiting for a very important person to come to the office — a Miss Gault."

Inspector Fletcher snorted. "Do they have good roast beef at this *Lambeth Inn?* Because if they don't Simon, there's no use in my going to the dive. I'm a plain man. I like plain food. I'm not and never was a gourmet like you. A mess of boiled potatoes, some rare beef and a couple seidels of beer meet all my requirements. That's provender good enough for any man."

"We don't provender ourselves tonight, Ira — not at the *Lambeth Inn*. We dine in lordly majesty. There'll be four of us. The repast will consume at least two hours from cocktails through the wine list to finger bowls. I'm not overlooking a single item on the menu. God willing, there'll be no raw beef, or any other kind of beef. Tonight you'll dine on the succulent breast of pheasant. You'll sip your Terrapin soup like a gentleman. . . ."

"Hold on, Simon!" Inspector Fletcher walked heavily around the end of the desk and placed a big paw on the private detective's shoulder. "I recognize the symptoms, and they're disturbing. When you're in this kind of a mood, it means that you're facing some dangerous situation which you haven't fully analyzed. You're expecting trouble of a violent nature very soon, and you're not certain where it's coming from. Right?"

"Right," nodded Crole.

"Knowing you as I do, Simon, I won't ask you to let me help you. I've still got a few more days to spend in this man's town, and you know where to find me if — if you need an extra gun or a pair of honest fists."

"I'll not overlook you, Ira. There's no man I'd rather have with me in time of stress than you."

"Let it rest that way. About that roast beef now?"

"Forget it. Esther will be waiting for you. Beat it."   ╲

Inspector Fletcher swore feelingly, spun on his heel and marched out into the corridor. The evening, as far as he was concerned, was definitely going to be wasted and frittered away. Breast of pheasant! Terrapin soup! He spat through the open grillwork into an elevator shaft and punched viciously at the down button.

At six o'clock Etta left in a swirl of perfumed anticipation. Left to his own resources, Simon Crole rolled a cigarette and swept the sheets of memoranda into a desk drawer where he wouldn't have to look at them.

At five minutes after the hour, Miss Ursula Gault entered, flushed and wet. Simon Crole got to his feet and helped her out of a tweed raincoat. She wore a rusty-black lace evening gown of antiquated style that looked as if it had seen service at the McKinley Inaugural Reception. An enormous Rhinestone ring bulged from the middle finger of her left hand. The white patch on her flat chest was achieved by a tremendous cameo brooch. Black, suede slippers completed the ensembled. They were spotted with muddy water.

"Charming, Miss Ursula," beamed Crole. "I had no idea you were so lovely."

"Flattery," scoffed Miss Gault. "Still, it's pleasant to hear someone say nice things about me even when they aren't exactly the truth. I know my face and figure probably better than ony other worldly mortal. And comliness is a virtue I have never possessed in any quantity."

He smiled unabashed into her moist face, then looked at his watch. "In precisely fifteen minutes we are leaving here for a night spot in Hollywood known as the *Lambeth Inn*. Included in our party will be Inspector Ira Fletcher of New York City — an old-school city detective of sterling worth — and Miss Esther Manning, a former operator of mine who has lately become a brilliant criminal lawyer. I remarked that you were lovely. Perhaps this sounds odd to you, and a little cheap. I assure you the compliment was not so intended."

"Thank you," she courtesied.

He placed a chair close to his desk and waited for her to sit down before relaxing into his own chair. "Smoke?" he asked.

She shook her head.

"Drink?"

"Not now, please."

He nodded reassuringly. "Miss Gault," he began, choosing his words with care, "it is rarely that I fall into error in the judging of character. I have, because of many years of criminal experience, learned to recognize certain unmistakable signs and portents which places individuals into two classes, the pseudo, and the real. Had I not thought you were a real human being, I would not have paid you in advance for something you may not be able to deliver."

He paused for a moment, then went off on a tangent. "Gene Scanlon had his vices, his faults, his kindnesses and his petty meannesses. I have them as well. But I believe he showed rare discernment when he selected *you* for a secretary when he could have had a younger and prettier girl."

Her smile was forced. "Please continue," she said.

"If that last remark hurt you, my dear, I'm sorry. Perhaps I can redeem myself later. My only reason for bringing it up was this: Scanlon must have seen in you something that transcended youth and prettiness, or he wouldn't have had you for a secretary. I'm merely following his lead."

Her eyes kindled. "Mr. Scanlon was a sinful, unscrupulous man. But he always treated me with respect and kindness even in moments of profanity."

"Listen," he went on. "How much do you know about the case Scanlon was working on at the time he was killed?"

Her bleak eyes met his squarely. "The police, the reporters, and others — all wanted the answer to that same question. Frankly, Mr. Crole, I don't know a thing. He kept the more important cases to himself. He even kept private records where I could not see or examine. Not that he distrusted me. He didn't. There was a lone-wolf streak in him that forced him to work alone most of the time."

"Was he by any chance working for a Mr. Gordon West, head of a large freight-trucking concern?"

"He may have been. Mr. West was in the office a number of times. Then something developed, or failed to develop. The two men fell into an argument. And West accused Mr. Scanlon of double-crossing him. I did not tell this to the police. It didn't seem necessary at the time they questioned me. Mr. West, certainly, had nothing to gain by shooting Gene Scanlon."

"That point is still veiled in obscurity. We'll abandon it for the moment. Tell me, did Scanlon have any operators?"

"Only occasionally. Whenever he needed a man or a woman for outside work, he hired them from the National Protective Agency."

"Are you sure that he had no one working for him — say in the interests of Gordon West?"

"I do not think so. In fact I would have sworn that no one was working outside for him until this letter came back as undeliverable." She got up, crossed the room to the chair where hung her dripping raincoat. From one of its pockets she removed a letter which she placed on his desk.

Simon Crole studied the name, address and the reason for the letter being returned. "Do you know the man to whom this letter was intended."

She shook her head. "No. We've never had a client by that name. And the fact that he addressed the letter by hand and mailed it himself indicates that he meant to keep it secret. Which makes me believe that he might be an operator."

"I observe that you haven't opened it. Legally it belongs to the Scanlon estate, and should be turned over to the proper authorities. Why didn't you give it to the police?"

"I don't know. To me it was the only record left of Mr. Scanlon's business. I didn't want to give it up. It was the only link that connected me with my former employer. And it's probably not the least bit important."

"There is," said Crole, urbanely, "only one way to find out. The end, in any case, justifies the means." Coolly he slit the flap with a practised forefinger and removed a folded sheet of paper bearing the heading: SCANLON DETECTIVE AGENCY: The message was typed and fairly brief. Crole read it through twice, committing it to memory. And there was no change of expression on his face at what he had read. Finished, he restored the folded paper to the envelope, and the envelope to his pocket.

"Have you by any chance been threatened, Miss Gault?"

"Not directly. A man came to my office this afternoon and suggested somewhat crudely that I'd better get out of the city. He was in the office when you arrived."

"I remember him quite well. Then you're not leaving the city?"

"I'm under obligations to you."

"Suppose I relieve you of these obligations. Would you seek safety elsewhere? I'm serious, Miss Gault. That letter you turned over to me is worth double what I paid you."

"I prefer not to leave the city. There is someone here who is dependent on me. And I really should be searching for another position when I have finished working for you."

"Your presence here may get you into difficulties."

"I'm perfectly able to take care of myself under ordinary conditions. . . ."

"The present conditions," he interrupted, "are not ordinary, but we can go into that part later on. Meanwhile, I'll see what can be done about transportation this wet night."

He dialed a number on the phone and jammed the receiver against his ear. To the man who answered the call he said: "Let me talk to. . . ." And at that point his voice checked as if he had been stricken dumb.

His eyes narrowed with pained concentration. An atavistic craving for physical combat caused the cords and sinews of his body to tighten in a hard knot. He felt a sudden, destroying rage — a rage against the instrument pressing against his ear.

But the fires of rage died as quickly as they had flared up. His body lost its tenseness. Cunning, temporarily deserting him, came racing back to help him. And the old scar on his cheek twisted his lips into their smile of perpetual surprise. The surprise, however, was real.

He wouldn't have believed it possible. Yet the substitution had been effected — while he was absent from the office. Admiration for the sheer audacity of his unknown enemies shone in his eyes. It made the problem more to his liking even as he realized with a sharp pang of dismay, that his position and that of Miss Gault had now become highly vulnerable.

So swiftly did these thoughts race through his mind following the cessation of speech into the phone that the pause was hardly noticeable when he continued with: ". . . the Chief dispatcher. Oh, is driver Scavillo around? Good. Send him at once to the office of Simon Crole."

Somewhat grimly he returned the instrument to its cradle. Then he rose to his feet, motioned Miss Gault to follow him, and led her to a corner of his office farthest removed from the telephone. To her he whispered: "Don't say another word in this office. If I seem to talk unnecessarily loud, don't answer. The telephone has been taken away and a different one substituted in its place. The exchange took place while I was away from the office. Wire tappers are on the prowl."

Humming tunelessly, he returned to his desk, opened the drawer into which he had swept the memoranda Etta had prepared, and scanned each item. There it was in Etta's neat handwriting: "The Bell Company had received many complaints about telephones being noisy. A service man, sent by the service department, came in and replaced your old instrument with another one. There will be no extra charge for the exchange. It's part of their regular service to subscribers."

He grinned ruefully. The telephone into which he had talked with friends and clients in the past was no longer on his desk. He had sensed the difference in touch and weight the moment he placed it against his ear. This new one was not quite like the old one, and it lacked a long scratch near the base caused by a fall to the floor.

There had been nothing wrong with his old phone. But someone must have thought differently. Hence the substitution. This instrument on his desk, he had every reason to believe, had never been placed on his desk by the telephone company. If he was right — and he'd have an expert telephone man check it in the morning — there'd be a tiny microphone within the earpiece that functioned even after the connection was closed. Everything spoken in the office could be picked up and transferred by a recording device to a phonograph disc. Which meant that no important conversation could take place in the office from this moment on.

He thought back for a moment of the things that had been said. Definitely, his conversation with Captain Jorgens could not have been recorded, for the exchange of instruments had taken place at a later hour. Only his conversations with Inspector Fletcher and Miss Gault could have been recorded. And the most important disclosure had been — the letter he held that Gene Scanlon had written to a man named Edward Corea.

Making certain the letter was safe in his pocket, he said: "Okay, Miss Gault. Time we were leaving. We'll continue our interesting conversation tomorrow morning. From now on we'll forget everything but the sinful pleasures of wine and food. You'll find the Inspector a forthright individual, a man of poise, and a rotten dancer."

She tried to smile at him and succeeded only into twisting her gaunt face into an unlovely grimace.

"Charming," he told her, again. "I had no idea you were so lovely." Had she been the cream of glamour girls, he could not have been more gracious and attentive as he escorted her to the street where George Scavillo's cab waited at the curb.

"*Lambeth Inn!*" he directed the driver in a voice loud enough to reach the ears of anyone who might be listening.

"Stepping out, eh, Mr. Crole?" grinned Scavillo.

"Into a large evening, George. Watch your mirror. Make certain the cab isn't being followed, then drive to the office of the late Gene Scanlon on Spring Street. Let us out at this point, and then keep circling the block until you find us at the curb again."

"Right," nodded Scavillo, hurling the cab into a narrow opening between a truck and a street car.

"The driver must be insane," shivered Miss Gault, "and you, too."

"Hardly insane, Miss Ursula, merely careful. Don't forget the switch in telephones. Beyond any doubt our conversation back in the office has been recorded for posterity by means of a microphone and a phonograph record. They'll know about this letter I mentioned as being worth double what I paid you. And it occurs to me that Edward Corea is going to become a pivotal point in the investigation. Of course they don't know that the letter was written to Corea, but they're going to be mightily interested in the letter just the same."

He peered out the rain-lashed window. "Have you any of the firm's stationery left?"

"Just a few sheets of correspondence paper."

"One will be sufficient. When we reach your office, I'll dictate a letter which we'll substitute for the one in the envelope addressed to Edward Corea. Should I be searched before the evening is over — and I should if my hunch about the microphone in the telephone is correct — I shall have had a very illuminating experience."

He took the letter from his pocket. "George," he said to the driver. "Place this letter in your pocket and keep it safe until I request its return. And remind me when you do return it that I owe you ten dollars for an important service."

"I'll remember all right," nodded Scavillo, stuffing the letter in his coat pocket. "I've got a memory like a bull elephant when it comes to people who owe me money."

They left the cab in a few minutes and entered Gene Scanlon's office. In a low voice Simon Crole dictated the letter to unknown Edward Corea. Miss Gault shamelessly typed it and forged Scanlon's signature. And the new letter was placed in the old envelope which he had saved for this purpose.

On the street again Crole took the girl's arm and dragged her into a drugstore. "Stay close to the phone booth," he told her. "I've got a call to make."

He dialed Police Headquarters and asked to be connected with the Homicide Bureau. To the man who answered Crole said: I want to talk to Captain Jorgens."

"Who's calling?"

"Tell the Captain that number Eleven is on the line."

The voice of Jorgens came over the wire. "Yeah?"

"Number Eleven calling."

"Go ahead."

"I expect to be searched this evening. And it is important that I know who is searching me, and by whose orders. Clear?"

"Yes. Where will the search take place?"

"At the *Lambeth Inn* probably. Can't be certain."

"Very well, I'll do what I can by having the place watched. You'll be covered. But don't expect too much." The receiver clicked. Captain Jorgens had hung up.

George Scavillo's cab was just rounding the corner when they reached the curb. He slammed on the brakes and threw open the door. "Where to now?" he called over his shoulder.

"Hollywood Boulevard — the *Lambeth Inn*."

Through the rain-drenched night leaped the cab, headlights almost useless against the glistening, black macadam. It swayed, skidded then straightened with a lurch at the nearest corner.

"An excellent driver," approved Crole.

Miss Gault bit her lips. Taxi's always frightened her. "I pray God you're right," she shivered.

CHAPTER 9

THE *LAMBETH INN* exuded a quiet elegance from its mauve-colored marquee to the appointments in its larger foyer. Dim lights created an atmosphere of intimacy and charm.

Inspector Fletcher and Esther Manning were already there when Crole arrived with Miss Gault. Introductions followed. The party turned their wraps over to an attendant in the checkroom. Host Louis met them at the doors of the main dining room.

"I am heart-broken, Mr. Crole," he lied, "but your request for a reservation came too late. The private rooms are all taken. I have, however, saved a table for you and your friends in one of our small, semi-private rooms on the upper level. There are only three tables in this room, and I am sure you will be very happy — and comfortable."

The private detective nodded. "I'm sure we'll be happy, Louis."

Even at this early hour of seven the restaurant was crowded with its usual habitues, eastern debs, horsey folk, directors, camera men, motion picture stars, and a few honest gourmets.

Louis conducted them up a carpeted stairway next to a platform given over to a Rhumba band in evening clothes. At the moment the band was playing sweet music. But this was only a prelude to the rowdy swing tunes that would later follow.

Two waiters entered and deftly re-arranged the silver. Crole helped Miss Gault into a chair beside him. A third waiter arrived almost breathlessly with a crock of *Pommes Soufflées,* puffs of crisp, salty potatoes.

"Lovely!" enthused Esther, reaching across the table and patting the back of Crole's hand. "Why haven't you brought me here before? Though I know the place, I have never been inside until now. The Inspector and I . . . the puffs are marvelous. Who's going to order? And what are we to select?"

Simon Crole tasted a potato puff, found it to his liking, and painstakingly began to write out the order. "Leave everything to Simon," he told his guests. "Nothing will be omitted."

"I came here to eat," broke in the Inspector. "And what am I served? Look! A dish filled with potatoes blown up with air."

"Observe," said Crole, unperturbed, "the menu. It is the very quintessence of Gallic art. I have eaten hamburgers with Inspector Fletcher years past when we both worked out of the Centre Street Headquarters. I did not enjoy them then, nor do I like them now. Against his will our Inspector friend is going to be guided through the intricacies of a dinner that begins with *Hors d'Oeuvres,* carried on through *potages, poissons* and other delectables, arriving after the correct interval to the item known as *Glacés.* Very possibly we shall have some rare cordials afterwards."

Crole completed the order to his satisfaction and turned it over to the waiter. As he did so he noticed that host Louis had come into the room. With him were two men in evening clothes. One was quite young, tanned and alert. The other was equally tanned, but considerably older. His face was square, his eyes pale blue, and he wore a clipped, white mustache. They both carried their shoulders well back, and the younger of the two waited until the older man had settled himself into the chair before he sat down himself.

Tiny creases formed between Simon Crole's eyes. The late arrivals did not look like any of the District Attorney's men, nor did they have the air of detectives. Yet there was something rugged and staunch about both of these men in evening clothes that he couldn't quite fathom. It troubled him, but did not lessen his appetite.

Later he beamed on his guests. "Well, it won't be long now. The *Hors d'Oeuvres* are completely disposed of, and I note that the *potage* is on its way in steaming toureens."

From *Green Turtle au Sherry*, the meal progressed very pleasantly through *Soft Shell Crabs sauté aux Aubergines, Alligator Pear* — and at this point conversation lagged. The waiters cleared up dishes. There followed a whispered conference among them, and then the pheasants were carried in, hot, brown and giving off delectable odors that even the grudging Inspector approved.

"Ummm!" he grunted. With a few lusty slashes of a knife he dismembered his fowl. "Not bad," he nodded. "Not bad at all. I've eaten considerable birds in my life, ducks, chickens, mud-hens, turk. . . ."

"Not mud-hens, my friend," reproved Crole. "They're worse on the palate than crows. Observe, if you can spare the time from that luscious breast meat you're shoveling into your craw, the general appearance of the two men in evening clothes. Tell me. What stands out about them in your estimation?"

Inspector Fletcher observed and said: "Sailors out of uniform. I noticed them when they came in. There's something about their eyes, the way they swing their shoulders, their gait — and the respect the young one accords the older — that definitely places them in a military organization. But they're not Army men. They're sailors — Officers, I mean."

"Excellent," said Crole. "Now listen, all three of you. There is more to this meal than mere eating." He lowered his voice. "Miss Gault is in actual danger. From what source I can only guess. My office telephone has been spirited away, and a trick instrument substituted in its place. This wasn't done to furnish me with better service, but to enable someone to listen in on private conversations both over the wire and in my private office."

"Hell, that's bad!" frowned the Inspector. "Excuse me, Miss Gault. I don't want to sound crude. . . ."

"I like," said Ursula Gault, "men who swear. My father was a master of profanity."

"Attend," said Crole, "to what I have to disclose. Whoever arranged the exchange of telephones must have listened in when you were in my office, Ira, and also when I talked with Miss Ursula shortly afterwards. During that conversation a letter was mentioned — a very important letter — one that was mailed to a man who was doing some outside work for Gene Scanlon. Scanlon, himself, wrote the letter. It was returned as undeliverable. Miss Gault received it and turned it over to me. And the people who listened to our conversation know I have the letter in my possession. Keep on with your eating, please, as if only mildly interested in what I am saying."

His eyes ranged across the room to where the two late arrivals were sipping drinks. For all he could see they were not the least interested in him or his guests.

"I expect," he continued, spearing an elusive piece of breast, "to have callers, either while I'm here in this restaurant, or later when I have returned to my apartment. And no matter what happens, Ira, don't interfere in the procedure."

"Tell me one thing," said Esther. "Are you involved in the Scanlon affair?"

"Slightly, oh very slightly."

"You must like to play with dynamite. Who's paying you?"

"That," said the private detective, "is a constant source of annoyance to me. I actually don't know — not yet."

"You're losing your mind, Simon."

"Don't be that way, my dear. Want to work for me?"

"If it's legal work, yes."

"I want you to take care of Miss Gault. She is not to go back to the empty office of the Scanlon Detective Agency. One unknown individual has already requested her to leave the city. And I don't want her to leave."

"Neither do I," said the Inspector. "And, by God, she don't have to get out of town. I'll take care of her. There's an empty room next to mine she can have. The *Manhattan's* a good hotel. We can talk to each other through the wall."

Ursula Gault blushed for the first time in years. "Why I couldn't do anything like that, Inspector Fletcher. It wouldn't be nice."

"Leave her alone," said Esther.

"She might be in worse company. And if she got lonesome and wanted somebody to talk to, there'd I'd be."

"The idea has merit," Crole observed.

"Nonsense," Esther protested.

"Anyone would think I had designs on Miss Gault," growled the Inspector.

Esther said: "Maybe you have."

"Miss Gault can trust me completely, up to a certain point. I think we'd get on fine together."

"There was some work I was doing in the office that seemed important to me," said Ursula Gault. "I was making out statements."

"Statements?" asked Crole. "I was under the impression that all books, records and papers had been stolen."

"I was making them out from memory. Already I had written thirteen statements when that man came in and suggested that I leave the city."

Simon Crole looked at her with a new respect. "You must have a very retentive memory, my dear."

"It isn't as good as you might think. I merely visualize the pages of the ledger and there it is — I seem to see words and figures."

"Photographic memory," said the Inspector. "I've known men on the force who were too dumb to make an arrest. But when it came to remembering license plate numbers, and the faces of wanted men, they never failed."

"Think back," said Crole. "Visualize all the people who came into your office to see Scanlon within the past month."

Miss Gault laid down her fork and focused her eyes on the wine glass. Monotonously she recalled faces and names.

"Those last two names," said Crole. "Repeat them please."

"Grandpaw Horschel, and Alvin Russek."

"Who's Grandpaw Horschel?"

"Charlotte West's father. But he was only in once, and was looking for Gordon. He lives with the family. The Wests have a son called Peter. A nice family if you like noise and confusion, so Mr. Scanlon once told me."

"Hmmm!" Crole pawed futilely at the carcass of the pheasant. "Grandpaw Horschel doesn't interest me. But Alvin Russek is something else again. Is he still the nominal head of the Civil Service Commission, Esther?"

"He *is* the head whether the records reveal it or not."

Crole scratched his ear. "That was my impression. A wise, distinguished looking gentleman, an excellent joiner, a civic leader, and a friend of police officers. The combination is unusual."

"Listen," said the Inspector, laying down his fork. "You're running around in circles. Berchtold is the man you ought to talk to. He *knows* something. And Gene Scanlon knew that he knew something when he was sounding off at the banquet. It's my guess that if Berchtold can be made to talk, you'll have all the answers."

"If Berchtold won't talk to his superiors, Ira, how do you suppose I can get him to talk? No, it won't work. It's too direct. I don't believe. . . ."

He stopped suddenly. Two men had come into the room with Louis protesting voluably behind them.

"Let me handle the situation," said Crole to his guests. He got up from the table and met the two men and Louis in the center of the room. "What seems to be the trouble, Louis?"

"These creatures," scolded Louis, "forced their way in and demanded to be taken to you at once. They said they were. . . ."

"Put a napkin on your arm," said one of the two men, "and start waiting on the customers. Crole is the only man we're interested in. Fade. We want to talk."

"That's quite all right, Louis," nodded Crole. He waited until Louis had returned to his station at the front of the restaurant, then smiled disarmingly at the two men. "I don't believe I've met you gentlemen before. I'm Simon Crole, and you're. . . .?"

"Post Office inspectors, Crole."

"Really? I'm glad to meet you, boys. But isn't this, er, somewhat unusual?"

"No more unusual than murder, Crole. My name's Herndon, and I've been detailed by my chief to locate a certain letter. The letter, according to our information, was written by Gene Scanlon. It was returned to his office after Scanlon's place had been robbed. Scanlon's secretary, Miss Gault, failed to turn it over to the proper authorities. The letter carrier remembers returning the letter. I want it."

Crole's eyebrows moved up. "Herndon, I believe you called yourself."

"That's right."

"Have you any . . . er, means of identification?"

Herndon extended his hand. In the palm rested a small gold badge with blue inlay. "That satisfy you?"

"Perfectly," smiled Crole. "I have the letter in my pocket right now. Miss Gault turned it over to me this morning. And it was my intention to place it in the hands of the police tomorrow morning." He removed the letter from his pocket. "There it is, Herndon. I'll be glad to cooperate with you further if you. . . ."

"It won't be necessary," said Herndon. "But I'd like to give you a little advice, Crole. Scanlon's death is being investigated by the proper authorities, assisted by postal inspectors. If you know when you're well off, you'll stop meddling with something that might hurt your reputation and feelings. In other words, get out before you're carried out on a stretcher." He nodded at his companion, pivoted sharply and left the room followed closely by the second man.

Simon Crole returned to his place at the table and sat down. "Ira," he said, "if there is one thing I can't abide, it's cold coffee. It paralyzes my palate." He summoned a waiter. "You can serve the cordials now, and some fresh coffee."

"Who were your friends?" asked Esther, casually.

"Postal Inspectors, my dear."

"They looked like a couple of hoods to me," grunted Inspector Fletcher, "straight out of the beer-running era."

"They told me," said Crole, sipping his Benedictine, "that they were Postal Inspectors. They even showed me a badge. A neat badge it was, too. Small, made of gold, and inlaid with blue letters was the design: F.B.I."

Inspector Fletcher snorted derisively. "That wasn't a Postal Inspector's badge, Simon. What that man showed you was the badge of the Federal Bureau of Investigation. Listen. The Post Office...."

"I am already aware of the shameful imposition practiced upon me, Ira. Deceit," he continued, thinking of the letter he had substituted for the real one, "is a double-edged weapon, as these spurious gentlemen will soon find out." He turned to the woman at his side. "And now, Miss Gault, you have seen the result of my telephone acting as a betraying agent. Those two men were undoubtedly responsible. Don't you think it would be a good idea if you went home with Esther and remained in her apartment until...."

"You really think they would harm me?" asked Miss Gault.

"I honestly don't know, my dear. I hope not. But our enemies may be just a few, and they may be legion with untold power behind them. The letter we wrote to Edward Corea may throw them completely off the trail. Then again they may recognize it as a forgery. I think," he sighed, looking at his watch, "that it is time for the party to break up. Ira, will you see that both girls get home safely."

"Sure. But what about *you?*"

"I have several places to go — all important. And if anything of a violent nature threatens to develop, believe me, I'll get in touch with you at your hotel. You take the girls and leave the building first. I'll follow a little later."

He went with them as far as the stairs, listened for a moment to the rhumba band, then returned to his table.

One of the three men in checkered coats got up from his own table and came over to where the private detective sat.

"Hello," he said.

"How are you?" nodded Crole, genially.

"My name's Van Sleet," said the man. "I couldn't help overhearing the conversation between you and those two men."

"I see," said Crole. His eyes lifted level to meet the other man's gaze. "So what?" he smiled.

"Perhaps," said Van Sleet, "I'm butting into something that doesn't concern me. If I am, say so, and I'll return to my table."

"It all depends," said Crole, "on what you have to say."

"Those men said they were Post Office Inspectors. They threatened you and made you give them a letter you carried in your pocket."

"That's correct, Van Sleet. That's exactly what they did. Have you any reason for thinking they were not Postal Inspectors?"

"Only a hunch. I saw the pair of them in the *Trocadero* yesterday, and the way they were drinking was something to marvel at. I'm not stating that Postal Inspectors don't drink. But I don't think they settle down to a siege of drinking in a public place."

"You're quite right, Van Sleet. I respect your observation and your logic. Also, your show of friendliness in reporting this fact to me. My name is Simon Crole...."

"Not the private dick who broke up the political racket in this city several years ago?"

"The same."

"Good God, you don't look the type at all. You look more like a — a priest. I always thought that private dicks looked hard, even vicious. You're a mild man." His eyes wavered towards the table that hadn't yet been cleared. "You're an intelligent drinker, your tastes for food appears excellent — I might say perfect. Yet...."

"What's your business, Van Sleet?"

"I'm with the movies. Maybe you've seen some of my work. Mad About Women, Sky Lovers, Paradise Forever."

"No," said Crole. "Unfortunately, I have not."

"That's definitely your loss. Well, I guess I'll toddle back to my stooges."

"Have a drink?" asked Crole. "Benedictine."

"Thanks." Van Sleet dropped into a chair.

"You appear regular, Van Sleet. I wonder if you could do a small favor for me?"

"Be glad to."

"Could you find out from the waiter who served those men at the *Trocadero* what their names were. Names, of course, can be easily assumed. Still, they help with identification sometimes."

"I'll see what can be done, Crole. Believe me, those waiters at the *Trocadero*, and other high spots, know more things about their customers than the customers themselves know." He signaled to a waiter. "A phone please."

The waiter brought the instrument and plugged the end of the cord into a fixture in the wall at the end of the table. Deftly Van Sleet dialed a number and spoke confidentially to someone at the end of the line. A short pause than he talked again, listened respectfully to what his informer had to say, then hung up.

"Are you on the level, Crole?" he asked.

"Absolutely."

"I'm glad to hear you say that." He lowered his voice. "Those two men are from the Blue Squad — Detectives Gonzales and Chambers." He rose to his feet. "If I were you, I'd watch my step. You're certainly going to collide head-on with trouble if you don't."

"Without trouble," smiled Crole, "my life would be empty indeed — and I should be very unhappy."

He watched Van Sleet return to his friends at the other table without actually seeing him. And the two men in evening clothes no longer seemed important. His mind was concerned with Detectives Gonzales and Chambers. Blue Squad men. And this meant that they belonged to a group high in the Department — an organization of picked men.

He sipped his Benedictine and waited for perhaps ten minutes, then reached for the telephone. With provoking slowness he dialed Police Headquarters and asked for Captain Jorgens.

"Number Eleven," he almost whispered into the receiver. "Any report for me?"

"Listen," said Jorgens, coldly, "the man I sent to cover you phoned in his report five minutes ago. He saw two men he did not recognize enter the *Lambeth Inn* and heard them ask for you. He followed them when they left, but lost them at the first intersection. I think, in view of this report, that you'd better drop everything. Sorry, but you just can't help me."

"Okay," said Crole. "I'll wash my hands of the affair. I thought for a time that I could help you. But I've since discovered the error of such fallacious thinking. Good night, sir." He returned the instrument to its cradle, dispensed largess among the waiters, and paid the check.

Serenity masked his face as he went down the stairs through a welter of swing music and dancing humans on the main floor. He found a taxi without much trouble and was driven straight to his apartment.

As he entered the room he sensed the futility of locks. For sitting in a chair, facing him as he entered, was a pudgy man with pink cheeks — Alvin Russek. Crole knew then that he was making progress.

CHAPTER 10

LEISURELY, SIMON CROLE removed topcoat and hat. "Hello, Russek," he said.

"Good evening, Crole. I trust you'll excuse my committing a minor offense, housebreaking. But I never did like to wait around in the wet. And I had to see you on important business."

Crole moved a taboret to the center of the room and placed Bourbon, soda and glasses on it. "I particularly detest house-breakers, Russek. Find anything of value?"

"I did not find what I came for."

"I see. Will you have a drink?"

"No, thanks. I will, however, have that letter Gene Scanlon wrote a few days ago."

Simon Crole poured himself a small drink and blinked at his caller. "I suppose, Russek, we ought to come to some sort of an understanding. Let's place all our cards on the table."

"The stakes are too high, Crole. Really, I couldn't risk such a move. You're calling too soon. What I'm doing is raising you."

"On what?"

"I have a search warrant."

"Keep it in your pocket. The letter you mentioned is really a document the Police should have. And being a civic-minded person, I turned it over to them. So it isn't in this apartment, nor in my pockets, nor at my office. So your search warrant is useless."

The eyes of Alvin Russek slitted so that they were hardly visible.

"You gave the letter to the police?"

"Yes — or rather was forced to turn it over to two detectives masquerading as Postal Inspectors, and exhibiting the badge of the Federal Bureau of Investigation. Actually, they were members of the Blue Squad. Perhaps you know the gentlemen. They must have taken examinations sometime in the past. Judging from the way they erred in exhibiting a government badge, they must have had considerable help in passing intelligence tests — especially with the local Civil Service Rating Board to which you happen to be connected."

"Who were these detectives?"

"I don't recall ever meeting them before, Russek. And the statement that they were members of the Blue Squad was merely guesswork on my part. Probably I'm wrong." He kept on smiling. And his smile was placid, almost smug. Wouldn't do to antagonize Russek too much.

He reached into his pocket for a sack of tobacco. Russek's hand dropped to his own coat pocket in a slow, caressing movement. It came away immediately when the tobacco sack came into view. Crole sensed rather than saw the fear mirrored for a split second in the man's eyes.

"Anything else you'd like to know, Russek?"

"I'd like to know who murdered Gene Scanlon. And it seemed to me that *you* might know. You were in his office this afternoon, took his secretary to dinner, and . . ."

"I didn't know, Russek," Crole interrupted, "that you were officially connected with the police."

"Oh, you didn't. Well, I'm not. But I am — since I hold a public position — very much interested in Scanlon's death. That's why I came here. I learned about the letter through the mail carrier. If a man dies suddenly, his affairs still go on — for a time at least. And that's why I thought of the mail. Only one letter has come, so far, to Scanlon's office. His secretary obtained possession of it, and gave it to you at your office. If you have given it to the police as you just stated, my interest in you is at an end. That's the way it is. Satisfied?"

"Quite," nodded Crole. "Will you have a drink before you go?"

Alvin Russek got slowly to his feet. He rubbed his hands together as if they were cold. "I'll make inquiries through the proper channels," he said. "The letter really interests me."

Crole said casually. "I read it myself and found nothing startling in its contents. Perhaps you didn't hear me ask you to have a drink, Russek."

"I heard you, but I'm not interested."

"You won't be interested in the letter either. Just a casual note Scanlon wrote to a man named Edward Corea about something or other. Not important at all."

"Edward Corea?" Russek stood close to the private detective — so close that Crole could see tiny muscles in his neck quiver.

"That's the name," said Crole. "Know him?"

"No," said Russek, fumbling for his cigarette case. "I don't believe I know him. I . . . I don't believe I know him."

"You needn't repeat, Russek. I heard you the first time. You don't know Corea, and that's that."

They stood for tense moments regarding each other, wills locked in silent combat. After a time Russek shrugged and started towards the door to the hall.

Crole backed up swiftly, opened it and bowed. "The next time you come to see me, Russek, you'd better bring a new bunch of keys. I'm having the lock changed in the morning."

"Might be a good idea, Crole, if you had your address changed. Chicago or New York would make an excellent background for a smart private detective like you."

"I dislike moving, Russek. There's too much confusion to it. Los Angeles is my home. I like it fine. Wouldn't live anywhere else. There is a host of honest and intelligent people here both in and out of the Police Department. And I'm planning to stay here, if for no other reason than to help them clean out the scavengers and crooked politicians who periodically fasten themselves to the city pay rolls."

"Meaning?" said Russek, blandly.

"It's difficult to explain," said Crole. "I know the police system in this city. It's one of the most efficient in the country. I know the men in charge of the system. And I know that they're basically honest, capable men. Pfui! This city is no worse than any other city."

He finally got his cigarette rolled and lighted. "And compare the homicide figures with other cities. You'll find them about the same in proportion to population. But in apprehension and conviction our police are way out in front. Murder is very, very difficult to commit safely in this city, Russek. Very, very difficult."

Smoke dribbled slowly from his nostrils as he watched the pudgy figure of his caller move down the stairs. He knew as he watched that here was a man he must not underestimate. Alvin Russek wielded a great deal of power. It might be well to get a finer line on this man.

Sighing, he removed coat and vest, padded out to the door leading to the back hallway, opened it and picked up the evening paper. Seated comfortably in the deep-cushioned chair, he scanned the headlines.

His lips puckered as he read: "Gordon West, of the Trans-Pacific Freight Lines, is being held by the police following an intensive investigation into the death of Eugene Scanlon at a Police banquet Tuesday night. West, at the time of his arrest, vigorously maintained his innocence. The police, however, are convinced that he has not told all he knows. Details surrounding the case are not lacking, and it is believed, by those high in authority, that West will be formally indicted for murder in view of the evidence collected by investigators."

"Ummm!" grunted Crole, closing his eyes. "I wonder."

For many minutes he continued to wonder, then picked up the phone. To the girl at the switchboard in the apartment lobby he said: "Get me the home of Gordon West, my dear."

The silence that followed was broken by a high-pitched, querulous voice that rasped from the receiver. "Dang it, who's a ringing this bell at this unmerciful hour? Hello!"

"Hello," said Crole. "This the West residence?"

"Suppose it is. Think I got nothing to do but get up in the middle of the night to answer fool questions? Call tomorrow. I ain't going to stand around shivering in my nightgown for any man."

"Wait," said Crole. "It's important that I talk with Mrs. West. Will you call her to the phone?"

"You talk glib enough. Who in tarnation are you? Don't you know night is the time for folks to sleep? Maybe you calculate that my old shanks don't get cold same as . . ." He stopped, cleared his throat and continued with: "You still there?"

"Yeah, Grandpaw Horschel, I'm still here."

"By God, you're a slicker. How'd you know it was me?"

"Your old shanks are going to get colder, Grandpaw, if you don't get your daughter on the phone. Tell her that I'm a close friend of Gordon's."

"Sharley!" yelled Grandpaw Horschel. "They's a slicker friend of Gordon's on the telephone. Wants to talk to you."

A woman's voice flowed over the wire. "Yes."

"Simon Crole speaking."

"Oh! You! I'd prefer not to talk with you, Mr. Crole. The talking stage is past."

"Listen," he said earnestly. "Your husband was in my office Tuesday, and . . ."

"I know all about his visit, and your refusal to help him. It's too late now. His enemies — and God knows he must have many — have got him right where they want him."

"Only just now," he told her, "I read the account of his arrest in the paper."

"Everybody will read it, and everybody will believe . . ."

"Not everybody, Mrs. West. I for one do not believe him guilty of the charge they are bringing against him. Not that I think Gordon West is incapable of such an act — I don't know your husband. Still, I don't believe he did it. He has a good alibi?"

"What good does all this questioning by you do _me?_ Or _him?_ The police found a revolver in his desk drawer — the one and only weapon that could have killed Mr. Scanlon."

"What if they did? That doesn't prove that West placed it there, or that he used it for a murderous purpose Tuesday night. The presence of the gun is unfortunate, but not necessarily fatal. I asked you about an alibi. Can your husband prove by unimpeachable witnesses that he was at some spot far removed from the _Commodore_ at the time of the shooting?"

"He was at his downtown office in the Terminal."

"Ah! Now we're getting somewheres."

"No, we're not. Mr. Jason Hertz, his partner for the past year, swears that Gordon was not there. And the word of Mr. Hertz is quite as reliable in court as the word of my husband."

"You're taking too much for granted, Mrs. West. You're willing to believe the worst when the worst, possibly, does not exist. Whether you trust me or not doesn't make any difference. I'm still going to risk my reputation on the chance that your husband was not the man who murdered Gene Scanlon."

Moist beads stood out on his forehead. He wiped them off on the back of his hand.

"I'd give anything I have to prove what you believe, Mr. Crole."

"I'm a business man, Mrs. West. Yet for once I'm not discussing terms. I never do where murder is concerned. I have not called you because I want you for a client," he lied unconcernedly, "but because I have a deep interest in the man who was murdered — a man whose profession was the same as mine."

He knew then that he had her interest — if not her blind trust. "Now listen to me," he went on. "I want you to phone two people. First, Judge Chadwick of the Special Sessions court. Then I want you to phone a lawyer — a Miss Esther Manning. Place the defense of your husband in her hands, and leave the details to me. You can ask Judge Chadwick any questions you care to regarding my reputation. Will you do as I'm instructing you to do?"

"Are you a friend of Miss Manning's?"

"Call her at once. After you have made these calls, ring me back. "I'll be waiting for your decision."

He closed the connection, poured himself a drink, drank it and leaned back contemplatively. The Wests, he knew, were wealthy people. He would charge them a flat price . . . No. That wouldn't do. It smacked of crass professionalism. It were better, he thought, thinking back on past experiences, to let the client set the fee for services. They invariably gave more than he might charge them owing to the fact that when the decision was theirs to make, they were afraid of paying too little, and so gave a great deal more.

The tinkle of the phone interrupted these pleasureable thoughts. He lifted the instrument to his ear. "Yes," he said.

"I have just finished talking with Judge Chadwick," announced Charlotte West. There was hope in her voice and a note of gayety. "He said you were notorious for charging large fees. What does the Judge mean by large?"

"I wouldn't know." Crole's voice was dulcet and smooth. "It's just one of the Judge's futile attempts at humor. As a matter of fact I make no charge at all. If what I do for a client does not satisfy, there is no embarrassment aroused by a statement of account. But if I *do* satisfy my client, he or she, as the case might be, subscribes to a free-will offering. As simple as that."

"Very good," said Charlotte West briskly. "I also talked with Miss Manning as you suggested and retained her as my husband's attorney. Everything is arranged. What am I to do now?"

"Nothing, Mrs. West. Absolutely nothing except to refrain from talking to police officers and reporters. Leave everything to my agency to handle. I'll call on you at your home the first thing tomorrow morning. Good night."

Simon Crole yawned heavily as he dropped the instrument into its cradle. Another day gone with nothing particularly accomplished. Three days in which to solve a murder that the police had apparently solved themselves.

He shuffled into a bedroom adjoining the living room, and shortly returned attired in gaudy pajamas and a flowered dressing gown. There was a half-smoked cigarette on the ash tray. He fumbled for it, retrieved it, and had it glowing just as the phone rang.

"Yes," he spoke into the receiver. "Good. Send him up."

He knew then that sleep was still in the future.

Matt Ridley came through the door beaming and dirty. "Hi, boss," he grinned. "It's Matt, home from the Punic wars, and choking from thirst. Ummm! What's that I see on the little table?"

"The taboret, Matt, holds Bourbon. Help yourself. You look like a stevedore who's been loading some ship's bunkers with coal. Haven't you any pride in your personal appearance?"

"None whatever, boss. I'm a working man, I am. Ah! Excuse the rush, but I'm nearly paralyzed with thirst."

He poured the drink down his throat, then settled with a grunt of content into a soft chair. From this point he examined his big, dirt-encrusted hands. "Talk about work, I've been a regular hog for it all afternoon and evening. I'm working at a freight terminal — or have been. I filled six trailers with cartons of canned beans, tomatoes, corn and spinach. I figure I lifted up and put down ten to twelve tons of vegetables for each trailer, and I earned three bucks. That's the toughest money I ever earned."

"Interesting," observed Crole, "very. From the standpoint of physical exertion, your labors have been truly Gargantuan. But I seem to remember that I sent you out to watch a certain police lieutenant. And now you tell me that you're a laborer. My memory also recalls the fact that you came back to the office this morning for additional funds to finance your investigation, and that Etta provided you with them. Are they exhausted?"

"Them and me," said Matt. "To the last nickel I used the additional funds your secretary, Etta, handed me to buy this job at the Trans-Pacific Terminal."

Simon Crole stared vaguely into space. "All this means something to you, Matt. But nothing whatever to me. You've spent forty dollars of the agency's money to buy yourself a job. And you earn three dollars working at that job. Where's the profit in all this?"

"I spent the three bucks for grub. I needed it, too. Geez, those poor freight truckers lead a tough life. Everything they earn has to be spent for food — or graft."

Crole's eyebrows moved up. "Graft?"

"I'll get to the graft part later," promised Ridley. "First, I gotta get something off my chest. You remember my report saying that

I was on the track of something big, colossal? Well, Jorgen's job is safe, and so is the agency's reputation. When you put me on the trail of Berchtold, I said to myself . . ."

"What's this colossal thing you're ranting about?" Crole interrupted.

"Gene Scanlon's killer. I know who he is."

"Marvelous."

"Gordon West," breathed Ridley, hooking his thumbs into the armholes of his vest. "Gordon West is the guy to turn in."

"Good God," sighed Crole, shaking his head sadly. "You, too, Matt?"

"What do you mean, me too?"

"The papers are full of it. West has already been placed under arrest. The police even have the murder weapon — or so they told reporters."

Ridley got up and paced the floor. "Geez, boss, I didn't know he was arrested. I swear I didn't. And I let the cops beat me to it. If I hadn't hung around that Terminal. . . ."

"Relax, Matt, relax. West didn't kill Scanlon."

"Yeah?"

"Yeah, as you put it. West was in his office at the Terminal Tuesday evening when Gene Scanlon was murdered."

"Does his partner Hertz support that alibi?"

"Unfortunately, no."

"Ha!" chortled Ridley, "then it begins to look like I'm right."

"It would appear, Matt, that your guess was perfect. The arresting officers searched West's desk at the Terminal and found a .38 calibre gun in the drawer. The press claims it is the one that discharged the murderous bullet."

"See?" said Ridley. "I tell you I'm right. Scanlon wasn't killed by the cops he threatened to expose; he was bumped by Gordon West. Want the motive?"

The eyes of Simon Crole blinked sleepily. "The motive would help considerably, Matt."

"Okay. Here it is. Scanlon had been hired by West to investigate a series of petty graft hold-ups on company truck drivers. Sounds small, doesn't it. Drivers were being nicked by traffic cops for ten, twenty or twenty-five dollars about once a week. You know, little things like lights not working, faulty brakes, not coming to a complete stop at intersections, speeding when the trucks were one mile or so above the limit. Fines were seldom paid in court. They went to the arresting officer.

"Maybe you think that's small graft. But the Trans-Pacific has over a hundred trucks in service, and the take runs from a thousand to two thousand a week on that company alone. Figure the other trucking companies in and you get some idea of graft."

"Keep talking, Matt."

"Well, Scanlon gets wise to the situation and kinda likes it. The grafters cut him in. West learns of it and loses his head. He comes to you in an effort to collect evidence against Scanlon. You turn him down. He's so mad at being double-crossed by Scanlon that he boils over. He figures Scanlon for a rat and acts accordingly. Can you blame him?"

"Under the circumstances, no. Where'd you gather all this information?"

"From drivers and loaders at the Trans-Pacific Terminal. I bought food and I bought beer. And the boys like it and me. So they told me plenty while we were loading boxes into trailers. It's funny, though, that I didn't hear about West being arrested. I don't know how I missed anything so important. It must have taken place while I was at the chili joint nearby talking to some drivers about the accident on Highway 101."

"Someone hurt?"

"One of the Trans-Pacific truck drivers. He was shot by a traffic officer he'd pulled a gun on. Some argument over traffic violations. He must have been a tough hombre to argue with a gun. So the cop shot him in self-defense. Ed Corea, his name was."

Crole roused up with a sudden jerk, every nerve in his spine tingling. And his eyes were no longer sleepy.

CHAPTER 11

SIMON CROLE'S first act on the following morning was to make a call on the superintendent of maintenance at the telephone company. To this gentleman he made a formal complaint about the exchange of telephones.

Then Matt Ridley came in rubbing his eyes. "Gosh, boss, I didn't know whether to report here, or at the Terminal."

"Go to the Terminal and earn three more bucks. And see if you can get a line on that driver, Ed Corea. Etta will give you expense money. Use it to good advantage. But don't use the telephone. And if I don't see you during the day, come to the apartment this evening."

To Etta he said as he put on his hat again, "I'm going to the West home. And it is not necessary that you tell anybody."

"I won't," she promised.

Behind Grandpaw Horschel stood the maid. Back of the maid crouched little Peter West, a wooden machine gun hugged tight to his chest. He was making a drumming sound with his lips.

"Morning," yelled Grandpaw Horschel. "Who be you?"

"Simon Crole," announced the private detective. "I'm calling on Mrs. West. She expects me."

"Hoho!" chuckled the old man. "You're the slick one who called last night on the telephone. Hattie," this to the maid, "go tell Sharley that Mr. Coal is here. Pete, you little scamp, shut off that noise afore I skin you all in one jerk. Come in, Mr. Coal. Just in time for some coffee. They's plenty on the stove."

Crole entered and was taken to a living room where a fire of eucalyptus logs burned in a large fireplace.

"By gravy," breathed Grandpaw Horschel, "Sharley is gonna need help." He looked at the private detective with the alert eyes of a bird. "Be you a priest?" He lifted a gnarled hand. "Don't tell me. Let me guess. Deputy Sheriff, maybe?"

Crole shook his head.

"Police detective?" The eyes of the old man were bright with anticipation.

"No. Private detective."

The light of anticipation vanished. "Never heard of such a thing. Can't be you amount to much, considering . . . well, here's my daughter, Sharley all gowned in silks and satins. Sharley, this here neighbor has come to help us. Mr. Coal, this is my daughter, Sharley."

Charlotte West extended a hand. Crole took it and smiled benignly. He admired the deep calm in her eyes. Behind her sidled the little boy, Peter.

The private detective removed a half-dollar from his pocket, bent down and placed it flat against the boy's palm. Feel it?" he asked, pressing little fingers together in a tight grip.

"Yup," said the boy.

"Now open your hand," said Crole.

The boy did so, and his eyes went sad. The half-dollar was not there. "I've been gypped," he complained.

Crole produced the coin from the boy's hair and gave it to him.

"Gosh," gasped Peter. In his eyes was an astonishing respect for the big man with the priestly face.

"My porridge is getting cold," said Grandpaw Horschel. "Come along, Peter. Sharley don't want us around while she's visiting with our neighbor." The two left.

Charlotte West sat down. "Gordon is still being held. What am I to do. If it's a question of bond. . . ."

"Gordon stays right where he is," said Crole. "I don't want him out — yet. I want whoever is responsible for his being there to think that he's going to stay there."

He paused. "Miss Manning will see him sometime during the morning. I called her before leaving for my office and instructed her to ask certain questions because I don't want to appear directly in the case. My reason for coming here was to ask you a few questions."

"I'll do my best to answer them," said Charlotte West.

"There's nothing personal intended in these questions, Mrs. West. It's merely that I'm seeking information. What is the situation between you and your husband?"

"We're quite fond of each other. Always have been."

"No divorce contemplated?"

"Hardly."

"Then there's no other woman."

Charlotte West's smile was pure serenity. "I'm afraid there is."

"I'm sorry."

"You needn't be. It's part of our life together — something I understand and condone. It isn't that I'm indifferent. He's a kind man, generous, and crazy about the boy. And the boy is the bond that holds us together."

"Has your husband any enemies?"

"He never discussed them if he did have."

"What kind of a man is his partner, Jason Hertz?"

"Reserved and silent for the most part. Gordon took him into the business when he expanded it a year ago. From what remarks he has made concerning Mr. Hertz, his partner is an able and competent man, well suited to the trucking business."

"Have you any idea where Gordon was Tuesday evening?"

Serenity still bathed Charlotte West's face. "Is this necessary?"

"The police maintain he was not at his office at the time of the murder. They have the word of Jason Hertz for this. Suppose they had someone else's word that he was elsewhere — a rendezvous, perhaps, with . . ."

"I see what you mean. It's quite possible that Gordon was in the apartment of Magda Lane." She gave him the street address.

He nodded. "Thank you, Mrs. West. Keep up your courage. I'll let you know the moment anything definite develops." He left her then and went through the front door leading to the street.

Magda Lane fumbled absently with the card she held in her hand and said to her colored maid: "What kind of a looking man is this Simon Crole?"

" 'Deed, Miss Lane," marveled the maid, "did the gen'man at the door have dark skin, ah'd say he look might lak Revrund Father Divine."

"I don't know," said Magda Lane, dryly, "whether the comparison is favorable or not. And it probably doesn't matter. Show him in, Sally. And don't go too far away."

She stood immobile facing the door as the private detective was ushered into the room. A woman of medium height with masses of soft, dark hair. She wore no make-up. She didn't seem to need it. Her skin was fresh and clear as a child's. Her wide-open eyes were the color of the sky at sunrise — a pale, watery blue.

Simon Crole saw all this at a single glance. Reluctantly, he revised his estimate of the woman. This woman was quality.

"Miss Lane?" he asked, a rising inflection in his voice.

She nodded, and her lips twisted into a crooked smile. "Be seated, Mr. Crole. I understand from your card that you are a Special Investigator."

"Bluntly, Miss Lane, in case you're not yet aware of it, Gordon West was placed under arrest last night."

Magda Lane's fingers began to pick at the fabric covering of the chair arm. "Arrested?" There was surprise in her voice, and the faintest trace of curiosity. "On what charge, Mr. Crole?"

"Murder! He is going to be charged with the killing of Eugene Scanlon at the *Commodore* on Tuesday night when the police were holding their annual convention."

"You aren't . . . but of course you're telling the truth. Your voice sounds sincere. Gordon arrested! How awful. Please, what does it mean?"

Crole said casually: "Don't you read the papers?"

"Heavens, no!" Her fingers continued to pick at the fabric.

The eyes of the private detective were on those nervous fingers. He wished suddenly that he hadn't been so blunt.

"I came," said Crole, "because Gordon West is a client of mine. He's in trouble. My business is to get him out of trouble. You're quite fond of Gordon West," he continued.

"Yes," quietly.

"Was he with you in this apartment Tuesday night?"

"Yes," more quietly.

"At about what time?"

"Eleven o'clock."

"Are you certain of the time?"

"Quite. I was listening to the ticking of the clock on the fireplace mantel and waiting for it to strike. I counted the strokes. There were eleven soft chimes. Then he came in and remained for perhaps an hour. I was happy having him here with me."

Crole said nothing.

"I'm not very bright," said Magda Lane, smiling crookedly once more. "Have I said or done anything that will hurt Gordon West?"

"Your evidence may not hurt him," said Crole, "but it certainly won't help him. If I could have brought forward a witness whose testimony would show that West was *not* in the vicinity of the *Commodore* at the time of the murder, then I would have accomplished what I set out to accomplish when I came here to see you."

Magda Lane said wistfully: "Then his being with me at eleven o'clock didn't help this alibi?"

"No. Scanlon was murdered at three minutes of ten. West could have killed him and could have easily reached your house by eleven."

Magda Lane did not hestitate. "Very well, Mr. Crole. I'll go to court and swear that he arrived here at ten o'clock. Perhaps that might be called perjury. But I wouldn't care. I'd do it in a minute if you advise me to."

"I believe you would."

"I'd do the same for any friend I loved."

The lips of Simon Crole twisted into their smile of perpetual surprise. "Your name," he said, "is an unusual one — one that has a curious alliterative quality which makes it sound like another name. The name is Magdalene, Mary Magdalene. Ever read anything about this unusual woman?"

"No," she told him. Her eyes of pale, watery blue seemed to be studying some spot on the wall not shielded by his big body. "As I told you, Mr. Crole, I never read the papers, books or magazines.

I never go to moving pictures. My only contact with the world is through conversation and sense of touch. I am, unfortunately, unable to see. I am quite blind."

Simon Crole had the feeling that his own eyes were not too keen to have missed this startling fact. He took Magda Lane's right hand between both his hands. "My eyes," he said, "will be sufficient for both of us, Miss Lane, until I can return Gordon West to the two women who love him."

"I wish I could see your face, Mr. Crole."

"Perhaps it's just as well," he said from the doorway. "I'll call the apartment the moment I have any good news. 'Bye."

She went with him to the street door, and stood facing the darkness that was for her blacker than night. And the crooked smile was again pulling at her lips when she closed the door again.

CHAPTER 12

THE YOUNG, rookie, patrolman, seated beside Etta's desk, jumped to his feet when Simon Crole came through the corridor door.

Etta said sweetly: "Boss, I want you to meet Terrance Doyle, newly assigned to duty under Captain Jorgens."

"Glad to know you, Crole," said Doyle, extending a hand that squeezed like a rock crusher.

"Be nice to the boy friend," said Etta. "He's going to be a part of the family in this office from now on, aren't you, Terrance?"

Before the patrolman could answer, Crole motioned the young man into his private office. "Walk right in. I'll be with you in a minute." Then to Etta: "Did the telephone man find the spot where the wires were tapped?"

"Not yet," said Etta. "Better forget the phone exists."

Crole shrugged complacently and went into his office. Doyle was standing near a window looking down on the street. He turned and grinned when the private detective joined him at the window.

"I'm new in more ways than one, Mr. Crole. But I'm working for a man whom I trust absolutely, and who trusts me in turn — Captain Jorgens. That's why I came into the office yesterday. We got separated, and I had to find him. Since I've only been on the force a short time, I'm under obligations to no one. Guess that's why the Captain picked me for special duty."

"I hope," said Crole, "that you're as loyal to your job as he is. It's almost noon, Doyle, and I've got to see the Captain. And I don't want anyone but you to know that I'm seeing him. Can you arrange it?"

"I think so. Where's the meeting place?"

"The Morgue in the Hall of Justice building. And make the appointment not later than one-thirty."

Doyle said okay and hurried out into the corridor.

Crole sighed, put on his hat and went out to the reception room. "Precious, roll a sheet of blank paper into your typewriter. Good. Now write the following words: An I ain't fraid of Ed."

She eyed him reproachfully.

"Do it," he insisted. "Write the sentence over and over till your fingers stumble all over themselves, until the words become jumbled and meaningless in your mind. Faster, precious. That's fine."

The click of the typewriter keys on the platen was like the faraway rattle of a machine gun. The secretary wrote line after line, slamming the carriage back again and again till she reached the bottom of the sheet.

"Stop!" he ordered. "Don't concentrate. Say the first thing that pops into your mind. What was your general impression of those words — phonetically, I mean."

"You'll laugh, boss."

"I'm not in the mood. Speak before you have a chance to think."

"All I could think of was *night freight* and *Ed.*

"Good girl. That's exactly what I hoped you'd think." From the doorway on his way out he called back: "If anybody phones or comes in, stall them off. I'm going to the Morgue in hopes of seeing somebody. So far as you know, I'm at the race track."

The Morgue was empty of visitors when Crole arrived. He sat down in a wicker chair in a room adjoining the Coroner's and waited. Patience deserted him after a time and he strolled down a corridor to the laboratory of the Coroner's chief assistant.

Without troubling to knock he pushed through a door. A small, lively man was at work on a marble-topped table. In one hand he held a bone and a pair of forceps. In the other a cigarette. He grinned pleasantly at the private detective.

"Ah! Simon Crole," said the lively little man. "Prowling in the

Morgue."

"Any new bodies brought in since Scanlon's?"

"A number — all of them accident victims."

"How about the truck driver?"

"Hmmm! Interested?"

What happened to the bullets found in both Scanlon's and the truck driver's bodies?"

"A question like that, Crole, is too official for me to disclose."

"Will you tell Captain Jorgens when he arrives?"

"Yes. I'll tell Jorgens. And if you happen to overhear, it won't be my fault."

"Okay. I'll be back in a few minutes."

He returned to the waiting room. Captain Jorgens had arrived, red of face and breathing hard. He said belligerently: "Didn't I tell you, Simon, that you couldn't expect any help from my office? And who put you in touch with Doyle? Damn it, can't I have one man in my office who. . . ."

"You have. Doyle is that man. He thinks you're some kind of a god, Captain. And I had to use him to get to you. My phone wire is still tapped. Probably you already know this."

"What do you want?"

"I'll explain in a minute. But first, let's journey to a room down the corridor. I want you to ask the chief assistant to the Coroner a single question. I asked him myself, but he refused to answer. He'll tell you though. He told me he would."

Jorgens said nothing as he followed the private detective along the dim corridor.

The medical man was doing something to the bone when the two entered. He sighed and abandoned it. "Well?" he snapped. "On with it. I'm a busy man."

"Ask him," said Crole to the Captain, "what happened to the lead pellets taken from the bodies of Scanlon and Corea."

"All right," growled Jorgens. "What became of them."

"They were placed in sealed envelopes, and at the present moment are lying on my desk waiting for a messenger to call and deliver them to the Ballistics Department."

"Your cue," said Crole to the Captain, "is to act as a messenger and take charge of those three chunks of lead. And don't do anything about them until I explain what I want. Will you do that much for me without grumbling?"

"Give me the envelopes," shrugged Jorgens.

"And if there is an empty cubbyhole around here," added Crole,

"I'd like to point out a few things that my investigation has revealed."

In a crypt, ordinarily used for the dead, the two men found perfect sanctuary. They seated themselves on a hard slab.

"Talk, Simon," said the Captain. "I haven't much time."

"You'll have all the time in the world if you lose your job," Crole pointed out, "and you're sure enough going to lose it if you don't listen to what I have to say about the murder of Gene Scanlon."

"Horse feathers! We've got the killer on ice. Even the gun. West is guilty. And the D. A. is going to make the charge stick."

"That part suits me all right for the present, Captain. West isn't guilty. That'll be proven later. Right now I'm not remotely interested in Gordon West. Attend while I recapitulate."

"It takes you so long. Say what you're got to say and be done with it. I'm a busy man. There are other investigations dependent on my office besides the Scanlon affair."

"I'm not exactly a slothful man myself, Captain. Again listen. Do you recall the words on Scanlon's lips when he died?"

"Sure. He said: An I ain't fraid of Ed."

"Something like that. I got to thinking those words over in my mind. They troubled me because I knew they were meant for you and other members of the force. And I become further troubled when I discover you're ignoring them entirely."

"All right. Those words interest me deeply. By God, I couldn't sleep last night thinking what they might, or might not mean."

"You're in one of those moods, Captain, which I choose to ignore. As I remarked earlier, those words troubled me. At times they seemed to mean something definite. So I decided on a test. I spoke them to my secretary and had her write them on a sheet of paper. She wrote them fast. And kept writing them until she had filled one side of the paper. When she had finished I asked her for her reaction. It was the same as mine — night freight and Ed. Notice the similarity in sound between *an I ain't fraid and night freight?* The word *Ed* stands out by itself, and seems to be complete, though it may not be."

"There is a similarity, but I think you're stretching sounds to make them fit theories. And they don't fit the facts."

"Not yet, Captain. You stick to *your* facts, and I'll attend to *mine.* But keep this in mind. Gene Scanlon was not trying to say with his dying breath that he wasn't afraid of Ed. That was merely our interpretation of his words. He was trying desperately to furnish you with some definite information that would trap his killer."

"Sounds screwy to me," shrugged Jorgens, unconvinced.

Crole removed his hat, examined it briefly, put it back on his head and said: "I'll not talk about Scanlon any more. I'll talk instead about Edward Corea. This man drove a truck for the Trans-Pacific Freight Lines—that's the company controlled by Gordon West and his partner, Jason Hertz. This man Corea was undoubtedly allied with Gene Scanlon. The letter Scanlon wrote to Corea, which came back to Scanlon's office as undeliverable . . ."

"I know all about that letter. There was nothing in it to prove that Corea was an operator of Scanlon's Agency."

"No," admitted Crole. "There wasn't. Corea may, or may not have been important as a witness. But he was suspected and feared."

Captain Jorgens's eyes became cloudy.

Crole resumed: "Corea was killed yesterday—by a motorcycle patrolman, just outside the city limits. My informer told me that Corea was supposed to have drawn a gun on the motorcycle officer. The officer did the only possible thing he could do—drew his own gun and shot the truck driver. Probably the officer will be exonerated."

"The two cases are widely separated, Simon. I talked with Officer Merkle who was responsible for the truck driver's death. Did your informer tell you that Corea fired first, putting a bullet through Officer Merkle's cap? Ah! That takes you off your feet. You thought you had me backed into a corner. Well, as I stated a few moments ago, the case is closed as far as you are concerned. West is guilty. And, unless he is able to strengthen his alibi, the D. A. will start prosecution. . . ."

"Captain," Crole broke in. "I thought you turned this investigation over to me."

"I did. But I'm taking it back. Right now."

"Too late. I've gone too far."

"Suppose I take you down to Headquarters and make you tell all you know? That's damn near a possibility."

"My memory can be notoriously faulty, Captain. No, I don't think such a move would help either of us. Besides, it's not worthy of discussion. Here's why. I have in my possession a clue that links the two dead men together in a common cause. It is a letter written by Scanlon to Edward Corea. The truck driver never received this letter. It went to an address on Hill street. But Corea had left that address. So the letter was returned to the sender."

"Ummm!" grunted the Captain. "Case history. It's unimportant."

"And the letter," Crole resumed, "reached me via Gene's secretary —unread. Whoever tapped my telephone wires learned of its existence, but not its contents. They determined to take it from me. And there's a curious angle to all this, Captain."

"Well?"

"Two different parties had knowledge of this letter. One learned of it by way of a microphone installed in my telephone receiver. The second learned of it through the letter carrier who delivers mail in the building where Scanlon had his office. Or so this second man told me. But I think he lied."

He paused and frowned. "This second man broke into my apartment last night under the protection of a search warrant. He was there when I reached home. But he did not find what he looked for."

"Who was he?"

Simon Crole seemed not to have heard the question. "Were Corea alive, Captain, I am positive he could aid us. He knew something. How much I don't pretend to know. The whole thing reeks, Captain, reeks villainy. Somebody's covering up. And that somebody has used a motorcycle officer to close the mouth of what might have been a very important witness. Edward Corea the truck driver was not killed in the manner described by Officer Merkle. He was deliberately murdered."

"Is that all you have to offer?"

"All for this session."

Captain Jorgens took a cigar from his pocket, carefully bit off its pointed end, clamped his teeth around it and said: "Senility has finally caught up with you, Simon. I knew that someday you'd have to bow to a lesser mentality than your own. Even your memory has gone back on you."

Crole blinked sleepily. "I bow to senility, Captain, but my memory has never failed me yet."

"The letter you speak of as a clue that links Corea and Scanlon together is out. I read it myself last night, and failed to see anything important in the message you attach so much importance to. Have you forgotten the two men who relieved you of that letter at the *Lambeth Inn?*"

"Years ago, Captain," drawled the private detective, "I read and remembered a wise observation by a man named Emerson. 'Life,' said this sage of letters, 'is a succession of lessons which must be lived to be understood. All is a riddle, and the key to a riddle is another riddle. There are as many pillows of illusion as flakes in a snow-storm. We wake from one dream into another dream.' "

"You're crazy," hooted Captain Jorgens.

"Perhaps I am," said Crole. "But not stupid. The men who received the mysterious letter from me were from the Blue Squad—namely, Detectives Gonzales and Chambers. They posed as Postal Inspectors and had the gall to exhibit the small badge of the Federal Bureau of Investigation. I gave them a letter, Captain. But not *the* letter."

Captain Jorgens said: "Oh!" He looked gloomily at the private detective. "So you recognized these detectives, eh?"

"No. I established their identity through a casual acquaintance."

"Suppose you give me the genuine letter."

"It is not in my possession at the moment."

Jorgens chewed on the ends of his mustache. His eyes remained gloomy. "I thought there was a catch in all this."

"There are several, Captain. And I'm keeping them for myself. What do you know about Officer Merkle?"

"He's never worked under me. I don't know him."

"Yet you're willing to believe his story when there is a faint possibility that he isn't telling the truth."

"I have to believe somebody."

"Officer Merkle's cap was pierced by a bullet. Was Merkle injured in any way—powder burns, or anything like that?"

"He made no complaint."

"Wasn't Merkle attempting to place Ed Corea under arrest when Corea threatened him with a gun?"

"Exactly. Yes."

"What was the charge?"

"I . . . traffic violations. Corea drew a gun . . ."

"Granted he did, Captain. Now. Were the two men fifty feet apart, twenty-five, fifteen. . . .?"

"They were less than three according to Merkle's testimony."

"The point is obvious, just as I thought."

"What's obvious?"

"Would you let me fire a gun at your cap from where I sit at this moment?"

"Not if I could help it."

"You'd be afraid of powder burns, wouldn't you?"

"All right, Simon. You win on that point. I'll have Merkle come down to Headquarters for further questioning."

"Have him bring his cap, and see that he leaves it with the Chief. But don't let him know that you suspect he was lying. I want him to think that everything is going the way he wants it." He paused and said as if it had just occurred to him: "Will you send Merkle's cap to my office by Patrolman Doyle?"

Jorgens nodded. "Getting back to Gordon West, Simon. . . ."

"When today is over," Crole broke in, "there'll only be one day left to find Scanlon's killer—one day, Captain. And there is nothing for me to gain by re-hashing what I've already pointed out.

"By all good rights I should let you go ahead and make a fool of yourself and your department. You're asking for it. For a man as intelligent in police work as you are, you can also be the stubbornest. That's your only weak trait. You're so damned scared that I'm going to turn up Gene Scanlon's killer before you can lay hands on him that you'd believe any story anybody'd tell you in order to make an arrest."

"I think," said Jorgens, with grim finality, "that Gordon West is guilty. Nothing you have brought out has caused me to change my mind. Anything else?"

"Nothing, Captain. And I hope you won't forget to send me Officer Merkle's cap as you promised."

"Anything to keep you quiet and out from under foot," sighed the Police Captain as he turned and walked heavily down the corridor between the crypts.

Amiable and serene, Simon Crole left the Morgue and returned to his office.

CHAPTER 13

GORDON WEST SAT behind a long table in the Visitor's Room of the city jail. On the other side of the table, but separated from him by a fence of fine-meshed wire, sat Esther Manning. She was watching him closely.

"All right," West was saying. "You're my lawyer. I didn't engage you. I don't even know you."

"But I know *you*," said Esther. "I know that you're in a dangerous situation, that you're being held for murder, that the chances of conviction are excellent even if you're not guilty."

"If you were a first rate lawyer, Miss Manning, you'd have me out of here on a bond of some sort. I didn't kill Scanlon."

"The Police found the murder weapon in your desk, Mr. West. Whether you placed it there or not makes little difference at the moment. As for getting you out of here. . . ." She shrugged. "That would be the wrong move. I want certain people to believe that the case against you is so strong that the courts won't let you out. I want these people to be lulled into a sense of false security."

"Smart woman," said West. "Who's behind you?"

"Really want to know?"

"I've got a fine, understanding wife, Miss Manning. And a grand boy. I needn't tell you, but I'm scared—scared that if anything should happen to me. . . ."

"Tell me," said Esther. "Did you, or didn't you?"

"You mean did I kill Scanlon? Lord, no! Why should I?"

"Any idea who did?"

"That's the same question the police kept asking me. I had to keep telling them that I hadn't the slightest idea."

"But you have—you must have some idea."

"Yes. I have many enemies, Miss Manning. They harass me and my truck drivers from morning to night; and from night to morning. It's just one long, continual pay-off to keep my trucks on the road."

"Who do you figure is responsible?"

"The police."

Esther leaned forward. "Names, please."

He laughed. "It isn't that easy. I thought it was at first. That's why I hired Scanlon to collect evidence. But what does he do but join the mob he was supposed to collect evidence against. I suspected him. After a time I accused him. We had a nasty argument in his office. After that argument I went to see another private detective in an effort. . . ."

"You went to the office of Simon Crole," said Esther. "And you suggested dictaphones and the like. You did not lay all your cards before him. Consequently he turned you down. I was in his office at the time. In fact I sat beside you in the reception room."

"I don't remember you," said West.

"You were too upset," she told him. "Well, Simon Crole has seen the error of his ways, and he is working on your behalf."

"The hell with Simon Crole," raged West. "I don't need him. I've got a good alibi for Tuesday night. I was working in my office."

"Your partner's name is Hertz, isn't it?"

"Yes. Jason Hertz. And he's a capable business man."

"Undoubtedly. But he made a statement to the police."

"He did? What did he tell them."

"That you left the Terminal at half past nine. At about three minutes of ten, Scanlon was shot. I hope your alibi covers those twenty-seven minutes, Mr. West."

"I don't understand," said West. "Why should Jason place the time at nine-thirty? It was nearer ten-thirty."

"It's his word against yours. Although he's your business partner, I'm afraid he'll have to go on the witness stand. And if he does, you aren't going to have any alibi. Mind telling me your reason for concealing those important twenty-seven minutes?"

Into Gordon West's eyes flowed sudden bewilderment. "Listen, Miss Manning," he said, "I haven't taken this arrest too seriously. It seemed to me a natural mistake on the part of the police. It never occurred to me that they'd actually accuse me of murder after studying the facts. Your continual reference to twenty-seven minutes is beginning to worry me. Can't you understand? There was no twenty-seven minutes to be accounted for. I left my office no later than ten-thirty and went direct to the home of a very dear friend whose name I don't want dragged into the investigation. I reached her apartment at eleven o'clock."

"Can you prove that you were in your office at ten—or near ten o'clock?"

"It never occurred to me that I'd have to prove it. No. I don't believe I . . . wait a second. There was an interruption around ten o'clock. One of the drivers came into the office through a side door which was generally kept locked."

"What was his name?"

West moistened his lips. Thought wrinkles formed in his forehead. "I don't know," he said, shaking his head slowly back and forth. "We have nearly a hundred drivers working for us, and it is difficult to remember names. I didn't pay much attention to him. It appeared he was having marital troubles. Periodically he'd get hurt on the head and temporarily forget things. This happened twice. During these spells of forgetfulness he married two more women. That made him a bigamist with three wives. I thought at the time he'd had a drink too many so I sent him home and told him to forget his troubles. He looked at his watch, made casual mention of the hour, then left."

"But you didn't get his name?"

"Sorry. I did not. However, my partner, Mr. Hertz, would recognize the man if I gave you a description of him. He has more to do with the drivers than I do."

Esther Manning's eyes narrowed. "I wish, Mr. West, that you'd say nothing of this truck driver, either to Mr. Hertz, or anyone else. I'd prefer to find out who he is by myself. And I don't want any—not even your closest friends and business associates—to know about this man. Please realize that if Simon Crole or the police fail to discover the identity of the man who shot Gene Scanlon, you are going to stand trial for that crime with the odds against you."

She paused. "What did this driver look like?"

"He was stocky, heavily-built. His hair was dark, and his face was tanned. I don't remember his eyes. They, too, seemed dark. And he was very talkative."

"Who brought up the time element?"

"He did."

"And what was the hour by his watch?"

"I don't exactly recall, but it was very close to ten o'clock."

Esther nodded. "I'll have to leave you now and get in touch with Mr. Crole at his office. Now promise me that you won't talk any more than absolutely necessary. And don't, if you value your freedom, possibly your life, mention this truck driver."

"No," said West. "You may rest assured that I won't talk—to anybody. How long do you think they'll keep me here?"

"I think," Esther told him, "that Mr. Crole has until tomorrow night to solve the crime. He's usually prompt in closing cases like this. I've never known him to fail."

"It doesn't sound reasonable," sighed West, rising.

Esther flashed him a quick, bright smile. An officer in uniform was coming towards them to return West to his cell. "Be seeing you," she called back over her shoulder.

West smiled grimly. "I hope so."

At the nearest phone booth Esther Manning paused. It was on her mind to call Simon Crole. Remembering the tapped wires, she decided against making the call. She'd go to his office in person.

He was sitting behind his desk when she entered, oblivious to all else except a tan gabardine traffic officer's cap resting on the desk in front of him.

"Simon," she said, seating herself near the desk, "I have just come from the city jail where I had a most interesting conversation with Mr. Gordon West."

Crole's eyes swerved from their contemplation of the cap to the face of the young woman lawyer. His mind was elsewhere. It was doubtful if he even heard her.

"Esther," he said, "take a good look at this piece of evidence. Officer Merkle was wearing it when he attempted to serve a certain truck driver with a ticket for traffic violations. The truck driver, evidently angry over the act, drew a gun and shot at Officer Merkle. The bullet missed Merkle's brain by scant inches and went through his cap. That's the story. What do you see when you look at this cap of Officer Merkle's?"

"I see a cap," she told him. "Nice quality of cloth. A cap that fits well and snuggles rakishly against its owner's head. And as I previously mentioned, I see a bullet hole above the visor. I also see a second one in the back. Now don't ask me to identify the calibre of the bullet that made the hole. I wouldn't know. Right now I'm interested in something else—our client, Mr. West."

"He's still in jail, isn't he?"

"Yes."

"Proper place for him. Off our minds. Won't hurt him a bit to remain right where he is. He'll appreciate his freedom all the more. The most interesting aspect of this case concerns—not Mr. Gordon West—but a problem in physics. Trajectory in physics, my dear, is the path described by a moving projectile. A bullet enters here," pointing his finger at the hole above the cap's visor, "and emerges here, at the back. The distance is short—a matter of inches. The trajectory in this instance would unquestionably be a straight line, not a curved one. Do you follow me?"

"My mind was journeying elsewhere. I know nothing of trajectories. My education has necessarily been limited to the commentaries of an eminent English jurist by the name of Blackstone. I have further knowledge of court procedure, the rights of the defendant, and how to select the right people for a jury."

"All right, Miss Attorney. At least you can think straight."

"Fairly so. And my thoughts are still on my client, Mr. West, who is being charged with a murder he did not commit."

"I'm not worried about West. Why should *you* be?" He squinted at her and picked up the cap which he placed on his head. "This," he said, "is about the way a traffic cop would wear the cap, eh?"

She nodded.

"Observe if you will," he said, turning sideways in his chair, "A perfectly obvious fact, keeping in mind what I explained about the trajectory of a projectile being a straight line. Now, if the subtlety of all this doesn't penetrate. . . ." Esther leaned forward and studied both holes in the cap, then placed her hands on top of it. "Hmmmm!

I think I see the light."

"Is it foul or fair?"

"Definitely it is not fair. The bullet went through this cap while it was off the wearer's head. It couldn't have gone through the two openings without taking a nice furrow of scalp with it had the officer had it on his head."

"In plain words, Esther, traffic Officer Merkle either held the cap in his hand, or placed it on the ground when he fired his gun. Why did he do this? To cover up the fact that he had used his gun without provocation. The truck driver did not shoot at all. It was Merkle who did the shooting. Edward Corea, the truck driver who was shot by Officer Merkle, was a distinct menace. He was working, at least part of the time, for Gene Scanlon. If Scanlon had to be wiped out, it was necessary that the truck driver be liquidated also. So he was! And that brings us face to face with a double murder."

Esther thought suddenly of the unknown truck driver West had mentioned. Her face went white. She saw the last prop of Gordon West's alibi being swept away in a blast of gunfire.

"I'm sorry, Simon," she explained, "if I seem overly bold. But if you have any Bourbon in your desk, will you. . . ."

"Of course," he nodded, still thinking of his neat problem in trajectory.

When the last drop of the amber fluid had been drained from two paper cups, he looked at her and said: "I'll listen to what you have to say about Mr. West now."

CHAPTER 14

ESTHER MANNING locked the fingers of both hands around her shapely knees.

"Simon," she began, "to use criminal argot, it is my conviction that you are being taken to the cleaners."

The private detective's round, sacerdotal face remained genial and placid. "Suppose, my dear, you relate your conversation with Mr. West. I've been taken to the cleaners before, and suffered no lasting ill effects."

Rapidly she sketched her talk with Gordon West, omitting

nothing.

He listened without comment — seemingly without interest. "You're slightly disconcerted," he told her when she had finished.

"I'm thinking of the truck driver who came into West's office around ten o'clock Tuesday night."

"Good old Matt will find out everything about this stocky truck driver who's worrying you so. He's working as a hired hand for the Trans-Pacific Freight Lines. He's already made friends with several of the drivers, among them was one he called Kleinhardt. Maybe, between them, they can ferret out your alibi witness. That make you feel better?"

"Oh, I feel fine. But I'm all a-flutter. As West's attorney I have certain responsibilities to face. . . ."

"Forget them and do something for the common cause."

She looked at him questioningly.

"Here's what I want you to do. Sergeant Beard is an old timer and can be trusted. Tell him you're cooperating with me and Captain Jorgens. Tell him you want the serial number on Officer Merkle's gun. I don't want any substitutions to take place at the last moment."

"I'll get the number," she promised. "About Gordon West, now. What will I tell him?"

"Nothing. Absolutely. . . ." He stopped suddenly as the warning buzzer beneath his desk sounded its tocsin. Etta, the alert one, was signalling trouble in the reception room.

The door opened. In walked Detective Gonzales.

"Well, well," smiled Crole. "If it isn't Postal Inspector Herndon. How are you, Gonzales? What can I do for you?"

"I'm looking for the Gault dame," said Detective Gonzales. "You've got her put away somewheres. I want her. See?"

"She isn't hidden anywhere. She's staying with me at my home. And she is being ably guarded by a stalwart friend of mine by the name of Ira Fletcher. If you discover that she is being held without her consent, you're welcome to take her elsewhere," said Esther.

"That's okay by me, lady. Just so long as I take her down to the Chief for questioning. Snap into it, lady, I got a cab outside and the meter is running."

Crole came out from behind his desk. "About that letter you took from me when you called yourself Herndon. Did it prove valuable to the Police?"

Gonzales scratched his chin. "Letter? Hell, it didn't mean a damn thing." He eyed the private detective with a modicum of suspicion.

"That was just a departmental mistake," he said, "same as my calling myself Herndon."

"And showing me an F. B. I. badge," added Crole, maliciously.

"Skip it," said Gonzales. "All right, lady. Let's go."

At close to five o'clock, Professor Hans Mueller, a ballistics expert engaged by Simon, arrived at the office. Crole took him into the small room adjoining his private office—the room generally occupied by his operator, Matt Ridley.

"Here it is, Hans," handing the expert Officer Merkle's cap. "Look it over carefully. I've already made a cursory examination. But it will be interesting to check my findings against yours."

"*Ach!* Turn on the lights. Go away. I should be alone by myself." He set his leather case on a table and began to take out certain instruments.

When he emerged from the room some fifteen minutes later, he laid a slip of paper on Crole's desk. "Vy I should gome here I do not gomprehend. There's is my rebort. I charge you nothing."

Simon Crole took five ten-dollar bills from his wallet and placed them between the Professor's chemical-stained fingers. "Everybody who works for me, Hans, gets paid."

He leaned back in his chair after Mueller had departed, and studied the report.

1. Exhibit reveals bullet hole above visor where pellet entered, and a second hole on opposite side where pellet emerged.
2. Powder-flecks on lower edge of visor indicate that at close range the wearer of the cap should have been mildly powder-burned.
3. Wearer, however, did not have cap on head. Soft material of same allows it settle low over wearer's head. Exhibit could not have been on wearer's head. Had it been, wearer would have suffered serious head injury.

Conclusion: Presence of scratches, sand and fine granules on lower edge of cap clearly indicate that exhibit rested on ground near oil fields at time a lead bullet passed through it.

> Signed: Hans Mueller.

Simon Crole pocketed the report as the buzzer announced still more callers at his office. His priestly face was inscrutable as two men came in—the same two men who had occupied the third table at the *Lambeth Inn*.

"Gentlemen," he bowed, "what can I do for you?"

"I don't exactly know—yet," smiled the older of the two. "May we come in?"

Crole indicated two chairs not far from his desk. He waited until they were seated, then dropped into his own chair, placed both palms on the desk top and said: "Well?"

"Are we free from interruption?" began the older man. "For what I have to say concerns our Government. My name is Courtney of Naval Intelligence. My associate is Lieutenant Commander Grey. Our mission is of necessity not of a public nature. It just happens, Mr. Crole, that our lines of investigation have crossed."

Crole withdrew his hands from the desk top and folded them over his chest. "Naval Intelligence, gentlemen, is a service that commands my respect. What do you want?"

"Information is what we are seeking, Crole."

Simon Crole said nothing.

"Information," resumed the Intelligence officer, "concerning the whereabouts of a certain high-speed motor stolen from a truck during a crash in San Diego. This particular motor was designed for Navy pursuit planes. It has a speed of eight miles a minute—probably the fastest engine ever developed by man. Should this stolen motor fall into alien hands, say Japanese hands, we will have lost a valuable offensive weapon. For other motors could be patterned after its design."

Crole's smile was enigmatic. "This is all very interesting and unusual. There is evidently some way I can assist you. But it hasn't occurred to me yet. You tell me that our lines of investigation have crossed. Where and how?"

"They crossed when Gordon West of the Trans-Pacific came into your office Tuesday morning. West was being watched because the valuable freight we have lost took place while in transit on Trans-Pacific trucks. They crossed again when one of our intelligence men, Edward Corea, was unavoidably killed by traffic Officer Merkle. We of the Naval Intelligence are not supermen, Crole. But don't underrate us. From the moment Gordon West entered your office, our men have been keeping you under surveillance."

"Are you sure I'm not in league with the other side?"

"Your agency has already been investigated rather thoroughly."

"I don't suppose there is any chance of collecting a fee out of the Navy?"

"I don't suppose there is."

"Skip the fee," said Crole, magnanimously, "and tell me something about Edward Corea."

"Is it necessary at this time?"

"Very," said Crole. "Edward Corea was not unavoidably killed by a traffic officer. He was deliberately murdered."

The private detective took Hans Mueller's report from his pocket. "I haven't yet showed this to the police. I hope you will make no mention of having seen it. Officer Merkle made the statement that Corea drew a gun, and discharged it at fairly close range during an argument over a traffic violation. The bullet went through Merkle's cap. Well, read it."

After a careful reading of the report, Courtney passed it to Grey.

"You're attempting to solve the Scanlon murder, eh?"

"I believe I've already solved it, Courtney. What's troubling me now is how I am going to prove it."

"You're an unusual man, Crole. What have you to gain?"

"Nothing that I know of—except, perhaps, prestige." He toyed with the idea of offering these men a drink, then abandoned it as unworkable. "Can you tell me," he asked, "if Corea was working as an operator for Gene Scanlon?"

"He may have been, but I doubt it."

"Then why should Scanlon be writing to him?"

"You have me there," said Courtney. "Of what did he write? Is the letter available?"

"The letter was written by Scanlon a few days before he was shot. It was addressed to Edward Corea, with an address on Hill Street."

The Navy men looked at each other significantly.

Courtney said: "He left that address suddenly at my direct order. And there again West fits into the picture. He, alone, of the Trans-Pacific, knew that Corea was a member of Naval Intelligence. I had to tell West in order to get Corea on one of the trucks. His orders were to talk with drivers, helpers and other employees of the organization in an effort to locate the stolen freight. He worked quietly, and unobtrusively. But someone must have guessed who he was. Getting back to the letter. . . ."

"I have the letter," said Crole, "but not with me."

"Can you quote any part of it?"

"All of it. But maybe I'd better write it down. It will save repeating." He took a pencil from his pocket and wrote:

"Ed: Report at my office. Bring all evidence you have collected. There's a leak somewhere. West plans to turn investigation over to another agency. Freight thefts have me worried. Somewhere in the set-up is another mob. I figure that the Big Shot and N. F. E.

are working with them. Expect to have that angle clear by Tuesday night. Be careful. E. S."

Courtney read what Crole had written and turned it over to Grey. To the private detective he said: "What do you make of it?"

"It's quite evident that Corea also worked for Scanlon. How the contact was established, I don't know. Corea evidently knew what he was doing and was not in a position to inform you. But Scanlon must have read the handwriting on the wall and became frightened. The initials, N. F. E. suggest an individual. Do you know any man with these initials in his name?"

"No," said Courtney, " I don't." He got up from the chair. "Mind if I keep this copy of the letter?" At Crole's nod he continued with: "I had hoped there'd be some clue in the message that would lead to the recovery of . . ."

"The clue is there," said Crole. "Only we haven't the wits to see it."

"We'll be shoving off," said Courtney.

He accompanied them to the corridor door and bowed them out. Returning to his desk again he sat down. The words in Scanlon's letter kept recurring in his mind like a nursery jingle. Sometimes they would weave a complicated pattern mingling with the last gasping sounds from Scanlon's lips as the doomed man stood beside the banquet table trying to tell what he knew before death forever silenced his accusations.

Perhaps it was merely a coincidence that the initial letters of Night Freight Ed and the reference to N. F. E. as an individual were so much alike.

Yet, if N. F. E. was an individual, who was he? Was there some unknown prime mover in the case whose name had not yet appeared? Crole's lips formed into a rebellious knot. He was almost positive that he held all the important strands of the murder web.

He sighed and reached into the lower desk drawer for the inspirational Bourbon. But inspiration struck him before his hand touched the bottle. He reached instead for the phone, thought better of it, and began to swear softly.

Putting on his hat he went to the reception room. "Precious," he told his secretary, "I'm going over to the *Commodore*. If Matt should phone in while I'm gone, choke him off. Don't let him say a word. By this time he has probably forgotten our wires are tapped. I almost forgot myself."

CHAPTER 15

I T WAS cocktail hour at the *Commodore*. Its three lounges were packed with young bloods, bored wives, picture executives and winter tourists. Simon Crole regarded them with a querulous eye. There was something raffish about the groups lined three deep around the bars that made him fretful.

His eyes squinched shut as a high whinny of mirth rasped his ears. He abandoned all thought of a drink and went instead into the tiny cubbyhole that was the sanctum of the head janitor. Into the surprised servitor's hand he pressed a folded bill.

"I'm from the District Attorney's office," he told the man, exhibiting his private detective badge, but not giving the man time enough to detect the deception. "And I'd like to look around."

"Yeah?" said the janitor, staring shamelessly at the bill and tucking it in his pocket. "What do you want to look at?"

"The alley outside."

They went out into an alley. Crole followed it to the rear into a sort of a courtyard. "Do they park cars in here?"

"Naw. If more than three drive in, none of them get out. It's too small to turn around."

"Were you on duty Tuesday night?"

"I'm always on duty."

"See anything suspicious that night?"

"Nope. No prowlers, no bums looking for handouts, no—say that's the night the cops had their party. Not much chance for bums or prowlers."

"Were you in your office—say between a quarter of ten and ten o'clock?"

The janitor took the bill Crole had given him and examined it a second time. "It's a V," he said.

"I might add another to it," hinted Crole, "if it will help your memory."

"Another guy gave me a V," said the janitor, "to watch his car down the street. Said he had something valuable in it and the door wouldn't lock. I didn't say anything about it because I figured it was nobody's business. I wasn't away more than fifteen minutes. Tuesday night, it was about quarter to ten when I don't have much to do. You aren't going to turn me in to the manager, are you?"

"No," said Crole. "I wouldn't do anything like that. Here's the second five-spot." He pointed to a window almost level with the driveway. "If anybody fired a gun near that window, you would have heard its report, wouldn't you?"

"If I was in my office, yes. Why? Did somebody fire . . .?"

"Yes. There was murder here Tuesday night as you probably know. The man who is responsible for the crime lured you away, knelt down by the window, and shot through the opening. Did you get a good look at him?"

"Yeah, pretty good. He rapped on the door from the alley side. And I came out. We went to the street together and he pointed out his car which he paid me to watch while he went into the hotel."

"Did you notice whether he entered the hotel or not?"

"I wasn't watching him."

"What make car did he have?"

"A Lincoln Zephyr. Swell job. Small license number XZ-99."

"That's fine," said Crole. "You're an observing man. Listen. When this man returned to his car did he seem anxious or flurried?"

"That's the funny part, Mister. He didn't come back. I waited until five minutes after ten, then got worried about being away from my post. So I went back through the alley to my side door. And that's all there was to it."

"Would you recognize this man if you saw him again?"

"Yeah. I'm pretty sure I would."

"All right. Keep your mouth shut. If I hear that you've talked to anyone else except high police officials, it's just going to be too bad for you."

"Yes, sir," breathed the awed janitor. "I won't say a word to nobody. I know when I'm well off."

Simon Crole left the janitor and went down the alley to the street. "XZ-99," he mused. "That ought to be easy to trace—almost too easy." His eyes slitted with concentration. That was a cleverly planned move on the part of the killer. The car XZ-99, of course, was a false lead to throw investigators off the trail should the janitor later be questioned.

As the private detective reached the sidewalk he almost collided with a Candid Camera man operating his picture taking business in front of the hotel.

Crole came to a stop and motioned the operator to join him at the curb. "How's business?" he asked.

"Just fair. I take a lot of shots, but we don't get many orders."

"How long have you worked this spot?"

"Two or three days. I shift around. Have to. The cops don't like the idea, so they keep us moving."

"What do you do when it gets dark?"

"Say, listen. I don't know you. And you're asking questions pretty fast. Why don't you say what you've got to say . . .?"

"I will," said Crole, blandly. "I might even order some shots provided you were working this spot last Tuesday."

"Shots? How many?"

"I'd take a print of every one you made Tuesday afternoon and evening—that is, if you made any at night."

"Sure I make them at night. That's why I picked this spot. Look at the lights. The sidewalk is flooded at night from the spotlights above the top of the marquee. I figure that I must have shot fifty pictures during the afternoon and evening. They'll cost you a quarter a piece."

"Go ahead. Print me a set."

"Just like that, eh? Where's the dough?"

"I'll go with you to the place where you print the pictures. When they're finished, you'll get your pay."

"Okay. Let's go," said the Candid Camera operator.

At a phone booth near his office he called Esther Manning. "Did you get what I wanted from Sergeant Beard?" he questioned her.

"I've got bad news," said the young woman attorney.

"For me?"

"No. For Officer Merkle. But it's going to give you a headache. The serial number of Merkle's gun is Y-25939. It's a Police Positive, calibre .38, purchased by Merkle when he joined the force.

"Routine, my dear. Where's the headache?"

"The .38 calibre gun with which Merkle shot Ed Corea was also a Police Positive. Only the serial number, instead of being Y-25939 as it should be, is Y-17642. Is that point clear?"

"Transparent as plate glass, my dear. In other words, there has been a switch in guns."

"According to what I uncovered, yes."

"I don't know what I'd do without you. Listen. Does West still insist that he left his office at ten-thirty Tuesday night?"

"I haven't talked with him since I made my last report to you."

"Have you heard of a woman friend of his named Magda Lane? Oh, you haven't. Well, you're hearing about her now. I talked with her this morning. She's blind. And she told me that West arrived at her apartment at eleven Tuesday night. You tell West that I've got to be positive about the time element if he expects me to break this charge against him. Good night, dear."

He waited a minute after hanging up, then dialed Police Headquarters and asked for Captain Jorgens.

To him he said: "Number Eleven calling."

From the Captain's end of the line came a moist, squishing sound as if the man had bitten off the tip of his tongue and was masticating it. "What do you want now?" His voice was petulant.

"Don't be that way, Captain. I'm thinking that today's nearly ended, and that tomorrow is your last day of grace."

"That's the least of my troubles. Chief O'Connor is sore because I let Merkle's cap get out of the office. Not only that. . . ."

"Listen," said Crole, grimly. "There's worse things than that can happen. I didn't call you to listen to your troubles. I've got plenty of my own. Now here's an assignment for your ballistics department which I am certain never occurred to you. Have an immediate comparison test made of the bullets found in the bodies of Corea and Scanlon. You have the envelopes containing them in your pocket right now, or you did have when you left the Morgue. Don't ask me why. Simply order the examination. Good night." He hung up quietly, wiped his forehead and left the booth.

It was raining when he reached the street — a hard, steady downpour. He bought a *Ledger* at a newsstand and plowed through the wet to his office. At the curb, some distance from his office building, stood an enormous tractor and trailer. Printed on the side of the trailer were the words: TRANS-PACIFIC FREIGHT LINES:

A stocky, dark faced man wearing a leather jacket sat behind the wheel in the cab. He was smoking a cigarette and staring into the shop windows on the far side of the street.

Crole kept on walking.

Lights glowed through the glass panel of the office door as he turned the key in the lock and pushed the door inward.

Matt Ridley sat behind Etta's desk, fumbling with the plugs at the switchboard. At sight of Crole he broke off the connection he was making.

"The hell with it," he said. "Hi, boss. I was just trying to get a call through to somebody who might know where you were."

"Are you with that truck down at the curb?"

"Am I with it? I'm in charge of it. I'm the helper. I load and unload, and make myself generally useful. The guy behind the wheel is Charley Kleinhardt."

"If that truck stays there five minutes, the driver's going to get handed a ticket."

"That wouldn't bother Charley. He's the damnest fellow for getting into trouble that I've ever met. He can make more grief for himself than any other man in this city. You know what he tells me confidentially, boss?"

"I couldn't hazard a guess, Matt."

"Cripes, the guy's a bigamist, and it ain't no fault of his. He got hit on the head twice. Lost his memory both times. And when he got normal again, he found himself with these extra wives."

Crole envisioned Gordon West sitting alone in his office Tuesday night just as West had described the scene to Esther Manning. A hundred or more drivers in his employ. And West hadn't been able to remember the man's name — only that he had three wives.

It was somewhat of a jolt to uncover a witness without having to interview all these drivers in order to track down a single bigamist. Bungling Matt. He *would* unwittingly do the right thing.

CHAPTER 16

MATT RIDLEY lurched up from the chair behind Etta's desk and came around to the front. "Sit down, boss, and I'll give you the real McCoy on this case. You ain't heard nothing yet."

Crole relaxed in the chair his operator had vacated. "That's fine, Matt. Let's hear the worst."

Ridley placed both hands on the desk, leaned forward and said dramatically: "West has a sweetie — a glamor gal by the name of Lane. She lives out on Sunset. I dragged that information from a couple of lads who work in the office. Boss, I sure had to ask a flock of questions, though, before that choice morsel came to me. Get it? West is a married man, and he's got himself a mistress. See? And Scanlon, knowing about this dame, tries to get his hooks into West for a big chunk of dough. Swell chance for blackmail. West don't take kindly to be shaken down. He gets mad — murderously mad. Get the angle?"

Simon Crole wagged his head slowly back and forth. "That's all very interesting and ingenious, Matt, but your hypothesis is based on unsupported, or ill-supported, theories of conduct. Now if you can get it straight in your head that West did not murder Gene Scanlon, we'll get on faster with this investigation."

"Pfui!" sighed Ridley. "Honest, boss, I really thought I had something in that angle of West and the Lane woman."

"It may be that you have, Matt, but not quite the way you have reasoned it out. What you have done is to confuse the chaff with the wheat — the wheat in this instance being your bigamist truck driver, Charley Kleinhardt."

"It don't sound right, boss, any way you say it."

"Never mind how it sounds, Matt. He happens to be a link in our chain. I don't know yet how important, but I'm going to find out. According to our client, West, a driver claiming to have three wives was in the office Tuesday night around ten o'clock. West says he left his office at ten-thirty. Jason Hertz, West's partner, insists that West left at nine-thirty. It follows then that if Kleinhardt can support West in the matter of time, he'll make an important witness for us."

Ridley scratched his ear. "The murder, according to your time, boss, took place at three minutes of ten. West says he was in his office at that time. Kleinhardt supports him. That would seem to make West innocent."

"Essentially, Matt, yes."

"How about the testimony of Jason Hertz?"

"Hertz is either mistaken in his time, or he's lying," said Crole. "I'd have you bring Kleinhardt up here for questioning except for one reason — I don't want him or anyone else to know that you are working with me. But I *do* want to know whether Kleinhardt was in West's office Tuesday night at ten, or whether he wasn't. It's up to you to get the information."

He looked at his watch. "You'd better get back to the truck. And Matt. Somewhere in this puzzle . . ." He lowered his voice and acquainted his operator with facts that the Naval Intelligence were interested in. "I don't know whether the stolen freight has been taken out of this country or not. Probably not, for all outgoing ships will be carefully watched. I don't even know whether these thefts are connected with the murders of Scanlon and Corea. Somehow, I cannot help but think they are. Keep your eyes open for any freight shipment that appears unusual. That's all, Matt."

The Candid Camera pictures, when Simon Crole examined them under a strong light, seemed to hold forth little promise. He had gone through perhaps two-thirds of them when he came to one of a man and a woman in evening clothes. There was nothing suggestive or familiar in the faces of either of them.

What quickened his interest were the two figures in the far background. They were emerging from the alley just as the picture was snapped.

From the drawer of his desk he removed a powerful magnifying glass and held it above the picture. The details became larger and slightly clearer. The man wearing the uniform cap was undoubtedly the janitor, the same man Crole had talked with earlier in the evening.

And with the janitor, unrecognizable against the darker background, was the man who had bribed the janitor to watch a car that was not his. Crole felt his breath quicken. And he knew now, beyond a shadow of doubt, that he was looking at the murderer of Eugene Scanlon.

His eyes swerved up as the sliding door of an elevator clanged shut. More callers on the way to see him. He scooped the pictures into the desk drawer and padded out into the reception room to welcome them, whether friend or foe.

He opened the corridor door. Facing him stood Captain Jorgens, grim, jerky, and gloomy as the wet night outside. Behind him stood Patrolman Terrance Doyle.

"Come in, gentlemen," said Crole, benignly.

The two police officers followed him into the private office.

Jorgens planted his body on the edge of a chair, leaned forward and smacked the desk with his fist. "Just why, Simon, did you phone my office and request that comparison test of bullets found in the bodies of Scanlon and Corea? Just why?"

"What did the comparison test reveal?"

"That the bullets found in the bodies of both men came from the same gun."

"Nothing more?"

"Don't rub it in."

"Odd, isn't it, Captain. Who's making the mistake?"

Jorgens's eyes became cloudy. He said nothing.

"I should have said," Crole resumed, "who's lying."

Still Captain Jorgens said nothing.

"It doesn't matter," said Crole. "But it was my belief, and probably the belief of everybody who read of Gordon West's arrest, that the murder weapon was found in his desk, and was positively identified as the only weapon that could have been used to kill Gene Scanlon. Either that statement made to the press was wrong, or it was right. If it was right, then your ballistic expert erred in making his report. If the statement made to the press was wrong, then someone deliberately gave out false and misleading information — information that is causing an innocent man to be kept in jail."

"We had to do something about that killing, Simon," defended the Captain. "The Department was in a tough spot with police officers from all over the country watching us. Though we did give out wrong information about the gun, we still believed we had the right man confined in the jail."

"What would you say, Captain, if I told you that a Police Positive .38 calibre gun was used to kill both men."

"You mean," said Jorgens, lunging to his feet, "that Officer Merkle . . . ?"

"I don't mean Merkle at all. I'm talking about a murder weapon."

"By God!" muttered the Captain. "Merkle, eh?"

Simon Crole took Merkle's cap from the desk drawer and tossed it to Patrolman Doyle. "Put it on, Doyle," he ordered, reaching into his pocket for Professor Mueller's report. "Read this, Captain. I had Hans Mueller go over the cap. This is his report."

Captain Jorgens read it, then glared at the cap on Doyle's head. After due consideration he said: "Merkle lied when he stated that Corea had fired point blank at. . . ."

"It's obvious," breathed Crole.

"But why should he?"

"Because, Captain, he did not shoot Corea. Someone else used the weapon. And that someone else is using Merkle as a shield. I'm not saying that Merkle is free from guilt. He's merely a part of a pressure group that is fleecing drivers and owners of transport vehicles. To be frank with you — and I don't want this known to anyone else — Edward Corea, the truck driver, was murdered, not because he was angry at being given a ticket for traffic violations, but because he was a menace to a second group of men allied with the group Merkle is a part of. To be more explicit, Edward Corea was a member of Naval Intelligence.

"Moreover, here's a point for you to chew on, and possibly digest. When Officer Merkle joined the force and the serial number of his gun was registered, that registration number was Y-25939. The gun he has now — the one used to kill Edward Corea — bears the number Y-17642. It is not Merkle's gun. You'll discover when the times comes, that the man who murdered both Scanlon and Corea is carrying the gun registered as Merkle's."

"Where'd you learn of the serial num . . .?"

"What difference does it make? You can place Merkle under arrest whenever you want to. Then pay careful attention to whoever comes to his aid. If nobody comes, put on pressure. He'll talk if he thinks he'll have to stand trial for murder."

"Damn right he'll talk," promised Jorgens.

He took a fresh grip on his cigar, scowled and left the office.

CHAPTER 17

SIMON CROLE looked at his watch. It was a quarter to nine. There were a number of things he felt he must do. Sighing, he got to his feet and looked for his hat. But once again the elevator door slammed out in the corridor. Heavy footsteps sounded in the hall. Fingers tried the door knob, then rapped on the glass panel.

The private detective walked leisurely through his private office and into the reception room. His priestly face revealed neither surprise nor embarrassment when he opened the door and faced his night caller. "Come in," he said.

Into the reception room walked a man wearing a new gray suit — the man Crole had seen in Scanlon's office. The same man who had politely requested Ursula Gault to leave the city.

"The name is Hertz," announced the man in the gray suit. "Jason Hertz of the Trans-Pacific Freight Lines."

"And mine," said the private detective, "is Simon Crole — though you probably know that much already."

Jason Hertz followed Crole into the private office and sat down squarely on a chair near the desk. "I don't know where you stand in this case, Crole, but after talking with my partner, West, I think you can be trusted. Wait a minute now, and let me do the talking. That's why I came here."

Crole nodded, but made no comment.

Hertz continued. "West and I hired Scanlon's agency for one reason only. That was to get evidence against certain men who were shaking our drivers down — and the men I'm speaking about were in the Police Department. It was because of this fact that we decided on using a private detective agency.

"It didn't work out. The drivers complained and with good reason. The cops had it on them — broken lights, loose wheels, brakes that had been tampered with. The drivers paid their fines. It was cheaper in the long run than going to court. Scanlon didn't do a thing to stop it. Perhaps he was unable to.

"Then followed several robberies of important freight. We both distrusted Scanlon by this time. So we agreed to place the matter in your hands. You turned West down. There was only one thing to do . . ."

"Wait a moment, Hertz. If you're going to tell me that West lost his head and murdered Gene Scanlon. . . ."

"I'm going to tell you no such thing. What West did, and I helped him, was to visit Scanlon's office Tuesday, and seize all his records in hopes of obtaining some information that would expose the ringleaders of the mob fleecing our truck drivers."

"When did you break into the office?"

"Tuesday night at nine o'clock."

"Then your statement that West left his office at nine-thirty was not true."

"Essentially, it wasn't true. My reason for making that statement was to establish an alibi in case we were suspected of being identified with anyone seen around Scanlon's office at nine o'clock."

"I see," nodded Crole. "To shield yourself and West from a possible burglary charge, you've involved your partner in a more serious charge — murder."

"That's it exactly."

"What time did you leave Scanlon's office?"

"About ten minutes after nine."

"Did you separate or remain together?"

"We separated. West returned to the Terminal. I went straight home to examine the records."

"Find anything of value?"

"I haven't had time to examine them. My office is in San Pedro where I have complete charge of freight moving in and out of the harbor, and all freight being transported up and down the coast. West handles the metropolitan area in and around Los Angeles. During his absence I have had to take control of the entire business. So my time has been limited night and day."

"Will you explain, Hertz, why you were so anxious to get Miss Gault out of the city?"

"I was afraid that our enemies would think she knew as much as

Scanlon did, and would use the same violence on her as they did on him. Purely a protective instinct."

"Who, besides West, had any knowledge of the military value of certain freight shipments entrusted to your company?"

Hertz thought a minute before answering. "Only myself."

"No outsiders?"

"None that I'm aware of."

"Still, somebody must have known."

"I couldn't say."

"Is West fairly secretive about his business among friends?"

"I wouldn't attempt to answer that one."

"Are you acquainted with Magda Lane?"

Hertz looked startled. "Yes."

"You knew, then, of your partner's attachment for the woman?"

"Yes. Of course."

"It's possible that he might have told her, isn't it? You know how men are. In an unguarded moment perhaps, he might have said something he shouldn't have said."

"Possibly. I can't help you there."

"I guess that's all, Hertz."

"I've told you all I know, Crole. And I'm sorry as hell that my statement about West is in the hands of the police. What will happen if I withdraw it?"

"I can't say right now. My advice is to do nothing, to say nothing. West is my client. He's in jail, but only because I have not yet found any way to clear him of the murder charge. What do you plan to do about those records?"

"Give them to you — if you'll take them. God knows I don't want them now in view of what happened to the owner. However, I feel considerably relieved at having had this talk with you. Do you want me to send the records to your office by one of our drivers?"

"No. Your drivers may be honest enough, but I can't take any chances. I'll send a cab with a driver of my own choosing. Tonight."

"All right. Here's my card with the address on it. Give me half an hour to get home and get the boxes ready."

Crole looked at his watch. It was twenty minutes after nine. "My man will be at your place at a quarter of ten."

Jason Hertz nodded, got to his feet and left the office.

Five minutes later Crole was making a call from a private telephone booth. In another five minutes Scavillo's cab was at the curb. The private detective told him what to do and handed him the card with name and address on it. "And I'll be waiting right here for you. Keep your eyes open. Don't let any car follow you going or coming. These records are hot, and very important to my agency."

"Aw, don't worry, Mr. Crole. They ain't nothing ever happens to this cab of mine. I know how to handle it, see? And how about that letter I'm still carrying around in my pocket? Haven't forgotten about it, have you? And the ten bucks you promised me?"

"You'll collect when you return."

In the interval following, Simon Crole entered a restaurant. By the time he had finished a meagre supper, the cab had returned. In it were two large cardboard boxes.

Between them they carried them to the office. After he had paid off Scavillo, recovered the letter that the driver had been holding, Simon Crole began his examination of the stolen records.

By morning he would turn everything over to the police. But not before he had gone carefully through Scanlon's entire correspondence and report sheets covering individual investigations.

If there were any report sheets covering the investigation of the Trans-Pacific, Crole failed to find them. Either Scanlon must have carried everything in his head, or Jason Hertz had already found and destroyed them. In any case, the answer was the same. There were no incriminating documents among the records.

By this time there was nothing left to sort over but a few dozen file index cards. Crole hadn't much hope now. He started an examination of the cards.

For a moment Simon Crole had no thoughts. He had nothing but two eyes that were focused on a piece of cardboard. On this card, in Scanlon's almost unintelligible handwriting, was the notation: *In emergency call T. P. EDmonston 3939.*

Crole laid the card on his desk and picked up the telephone book. Opening it he turned section T. He found Trans-Pacific without any trouble. Listed under Terminal were three telephone numbers under headings of Office, Warehouse, and Chief Dispatcher. But underneath these listings was still another — the elusive key that unlocked the cryptic cipher and made everything simple as it had been from the beginning.

He closed the book, tucked the card in his pocket and stared bemusedly at the wall. After a time a tired, tricky smile bathed his priestly face. There was not the slightest hesitation in movements as he scooped the telephone from his desk and dialed Police Headquarters.

"Is Captain Jorgens there?" he asked. "Oh, he isn't. I see. Well, I'll leave a message for him. Never mind who this is calling. Simply tell Captain Jorgens that the records missing from Gene Scanlon's office have been recovered. That's right. They're in the office of Simon Crole. And if the Captain is still interested in them he can send for them in the morning. That's right. Office of Simon Crole. The Captain will understand."

He broke the connection and made a second call. This call went to the switchboard operator in the building where he had his apartment. To the night operator he said: "Simon Crole speaking. Any calls for me? All right. You can tell me when I reach home. I'm leaving the office at once. Had a rotten day. This business is getting me down. That's all. Good night, my dear."

The same tricky smile was on his face when he heard a distant click somewheres along the telephone wires. The tappers were still at their post. And he knew then that his unseen listeners had finally heard something — something he had determined they should hear.

Crole wasted no time. Switching off all lights, he sat down at his desk to await nocturnal callers. He did not mind waiting alone in the dark.

The elevators had long since stopped running. If anyone came — and he knew that someone *would* come — he would have ample warning. Long minutes dragged. He left his desk and went to the window where he could look down to the street.

The car, when he saw it, was coming slowly around the corner and stopping near the curb across the street. Two men got out and looked up at the darkened windows of the building. Crole edged back into the room. Long before the two men had climbed the last flight of stairs and were scratching with master keys at the lock, the private detective had entered the washroom and bolted the door.

He could not see them when they finally unlocked the door and entered the reception room. But he could hear the low murmur of their voices. They switched on the lights. It was then that he saw them clearly — Detectives Gonzales and Chambers.

They pounced upon the Scanlon loot like carrion birds on a stricken rabbit. In less than five minutes they had the records back in the boxes and were on their way out. Chambers switched off the lights and clicked the door shut.

Crole left his hiding place fast, scrambled through a window near Etta's desk and moved catlike down the fire-escape. He re-entered the building on the first floor and stood listening to their footsteps above him. Down the remaining flight he moved, through the entrance hall and into the night.

By the time they reached the street and had carried the boxes to their car, Crole had found a night-cruising taxi. To the hacker he said: "Follow that car." He pointed it out. The police machine was moving swiftly from the curb. "And it's worth ten dollars to me if you don't lose it."

"Right," nodded the driver. "Did you know you're tailing a squad car?"

"Yes, I know. So don't ask questions. I'm connected with the police myself."

"The hell!" spat the driver.

"Forget it," Crole said. "You're being paid the limit."

They trailed the squad car for a number of blocks where it finally swerved up the ramp of an all-night garage.

"Drive on past," ordered the private detective. "Slow. I want a good look at that garage."

When the cab had passed the ramp up which the car had climbed and vanished, Crole gave an address close to his apartment. From this point he walked to the building.

Matt Ridley was talking to the night operator when Crole came in. He looked tired, and his face was incredibly dirty. His grin, however, was spontaneous. "Hiyah, boss."

Crole said to the operator: "That call you told me about?"

"It was from Miss Manning. She said she'd phone again, or come to the apartment and wait."

He nodded and motioned Ridley up the stairs. In the sanctuary of his rooms he said: "Find out anything?"

"Not from Kleinhardt. I tried to pump him about Ed Corea. But he didn't know a thing. Wednesday was his day off. He wasn't working."

"I'm thinking about Tuesday night."

"Oh. Geez, I forgot to ask him. Russek was down at the Terminal. He had a moll with him. Good looking jane, but she had funny eyes."

"Funny? In what way?"

"I don't know. She didn't seem to be looking at anything in particular as she sat in his car, but I had the feeling she was watching me and Charley while we were loading a trailer."

"What was Russek doing at the Terminal?"

"I couldn't find out. He talked with Kleinhardt a few seconds while I was loading a handtruck. I afterwards asked Charley who his friends were. He said he didn't know them — just some people asking about Gordon West."

Crole's eyelids began to droop. "Call George Scavillo," he said abruptly. "You and I are going for a ride. We're going out on Sunset Boulevard and visit, and possibly burglarize, the apartment of a beautiful woman — a confidante of Gordon West."

CHAPTER 18

PARALLEL to Sunset Boulevard, but many feet higher, curved Highby Drive in a region of Cape God and pseudo-colonial houses. Here, beneath a sprawling pepper tree, George Scavillo stopped his machine.

Simon Crole stepped to the roadway with Ridley close behind him.

Wet weeds slapped against their legs as they crossed a vacant lot and began to slip and slide down the sharp slant of a hill. Below them was an apartment building, its stuccoed walls rising ghostly and white against the shadows of night.

When they stopped at a Cypress hedge, they had a close view of all the windows on one side of the building.

"There is the place," said Crole. "And somehow we've got to get inside. There are only two apartments in the building. Miss Lane had the one on this side. She has a colored maid, and the maid undoubtedly lives with her. Look. There's a car standing in the drive. Can you identify it?"

"Looks," said Ridley, squinting through the dark, "like the one Russek was using this afternoon."

"That rather complicates things for the moment," sighed Crole. "I wish Russek was somewheres else."

"Hell," spat Ridley. "I'll take him out."

"It isn't that simple, Matt. No, we'll have to wait until he leaves of his own accord. Go back up the hill and get in Scavillo's cab. Have George park close so you can watch the car. Then follow Russek when he leaves. Don't let him out of your sight for a moment. I'm staying here alone."

Ridley nodded and climbed the hill to the Drive where Scavillo's cab was parked.

Pudgy, pink-cheeked Alvin Russek sat in a chair facing Magda Lane. There was a queer glint in his eyes as he sat watching her.

The soft curves of her body pleased him, and the longing to possess her was slowly undermining all the barriers he had built to shield his shady activities.

"Why so quiet all of a sudden?" she asked.

"I was thinking," he said. "Mind if I use the phone?"

Russek called a number, talked and listened for perhaps five minutes, then set the instrument back on a table near the wall.

"What is it?" she asked, casually.

"Gonzales caught that private detective off guard. Crole said too much over the telephone. Scanlon's records were in his office. So he and Chambers went down and broke in. All the incriminating evidence Scanlon had collected against me is now in ashes. That was a good break."

"It sounds very exciting. Aren't you afraid . . .?"

"Of what?" He tried to forget that he was a pudgy man on the wrong side of forty. He was concerned only with impressing this strange and desirable woman. "The police picked up Merkle. You remember me telling you about that traffic officer. They questioned him once before. Now they're going to question him again. A matter of gun numbers. The one he had in his possession wasn't the weapon he was supposed to have according to the serial number registration."

"You certainly are involved in a great many enterprises. There are times when I feel I should be afraid of you, Alvin."

"I don't want you to be, Magda."

"Nor do I want to. In this dark world I live in, Alvin, I want you for a friend, a very dear friend, one I can trust, and one who will trust me."

He came over to where she sat. She felt his nearness and rose to her feet. "Afraid I can't stay much longer. It's urgent that I go down to Police Headquarters and see what I can do to help Merkle."

"Is it not possible," said Magda Lane, "that the police have purposely brought Merkle to Headquarters this second time—as a kind of a trap that would reveal who his friends are?"

He looked approvingly at her wide, unseeing eyes. "That's a thought. A damned good thought. I'll think it over. You may be right. Maybe I won't go down to Headquarters after all. But there are other things that must be attended to. I hate to leave you. . . ."

"There are going to be other nights, Alvin," she told him, taking his arm and going with him to the street door. "Yes, there are going to be a great many nights in the years stretching out before you."

Something in the way she spoke disturbed him. Why this was he did not know. Perhaps it wasn't her voice, after all — merely the words she had used. Somehow they sounded like the impersonal drone of a judge pronouncing sentence—years stretching out before you.

He thrust the feeling aside and gathered her body into his arms. She was passive, soft. She lacked fire. He released her suddenly.

"Good night," he said, gruffly.

Her voice was tender. "Good night, Alvin."

A few moments later he backed his car from the driveway and drove swiftly down Sunset Boulevard. And behind his machine trailed the cab of George Scavillo.

When Russek left his car to enter one of a row of phone booths in a downtown drugstore, Matt Ridley eased inconspicuously into the booth adjoining. Ear pressed tightly against the thin partition separating the booths, he listened to everything Russek had to say.

His face was grim when he sauntered from the booth and returned to Scavillo's cab. He wondered whether he should abandon Russek at this point and contact Crole again. He decided to stick to Russek and phone Crole later, or the first thing in the morning.

From his point of vantage on the high embankment, Simon Crole saw the car back from the drive. He wasted little thought on Russek now, his attention being centered on the apartment and possible length of time necessary before he could safely enter it.

The lights on the lower floor winked out. Then to his amazement they came on in a room facing the spot where he watched. The shades were only partly drawn and the private detective could see the woman moving about the room in a blue peignoir. Even as he watched, the shades were completely drawn down cutting off her further movements.

The drawing of the shades was not important. The important thing was that she had turned on the lights. The action was a betrayal—an acknowledgment that light was necessary. And light shouldn't have been necessary to one who lived constantly in the dark.

Simon Crole's lips twisted into their smile of perpetual surprise. Magda Lane had to have light in order to see. Magda Lane was not blind.

Crouching in the wet dark, Simon Crole again visualized the eyes that had been so close to his when he had visited her apartment. Those eyes he had seen were sightless. Of that he was positive. There was in them only a steady, unblinking, unseeing stare so characteristic of the blind. They were as cold, as emotionless as marbles—as glass.

The lights behind the shades went out after a while. And when he thought she must surely be asleep, he walked softly up the concrete steps to the front door.

With the silence and deftness of a cracksman he fitted keys into the lock until one of them slid back the lock bolt. He opened the door, stepped into the hall and closed it soundlessly behind him.

Up the stairs he moved, a huge bulk of dark fluidity, placing his weight on the outer edge of the stairs to eliminate any creak. In the hall above he dropped to his knees and explored the walls on both sides with his fingers.

The door to her room, when he reached it, was open. Her quiet, regular breathing was barely audible.

Slowly, inexorably, Simon Crole crawled towards a dressing table beside a window. And his hunched, moving body was like that of a great cat stalking unwary prey.

Another inch flowed beneath his moving body, and another, until their steady accumulation added up to the distance from the door to the dressing table. His first goal had been reached. Would he have to search further, or would he find what he hoped to find within reach of his fingers?

Lightly, as though his fingers had no more substance than shadows, he touched each article on the dresser, beginning at one end and working towards the other. Perfume bottles, lotions, brushes, comb, compact jars, each bringing a definite picture to his mind. His exploring fingers came then to a purse, felt it, discarded it, and moved relentlessly onward until they encountered two objects that felt like individual halves of very small egg shells. They rested on a pad of soft cotton.

Magda Lane turned uneasily in her bed.

The private detective froze into stark immobility. When her breathing had returned to its former rhythm, he reached up to the dressing table top and removed one of the two objects resting on the cotton pad, and placed it carefully in his vest pocket. Then, with the same lack of haste in which he had entered the bedroom, he crawled slowly and soundlessly out of it.

Though she did not know it, and would not know it until morning, Magda Lane's home had been burglarized. But only one thing had been disturbed—the cotton pad. And even that could hardly have been called disturbed. Deprived, rather, of something very delicate, very personal, and decidedly incriminating.

The night operator at Crole's apartment building turned from her switchboard when the private detective entered the lobby.

"Miss Manning phoned again, and I think she is on her way to the apartment."

"Thank you, my dear," said Crole, folding a bill and placing it in her hand where it lay on the switchboard.

Slowly he toiled up the stairs to his apartment. The phone was ringing as he entered. Esther had arrived. She was in the lobby downstairs. He told the operator to send her up. Leaving the door unlocked, he removed his hat and coat, and put on a dressing gown.

"You're soaking wet," she told him, standing her dripping umbrella in a corner.

He smiled. "I've been on a nocturnal expedition on Sunset Boulevard. Been prowling around in the mud and wet, and it's natural that I should have absorbed some moisture."

"What else are you guilty of?"

"Illegal entry into a building. A minor theft. I was seeking evidence."

"Then you must have found what you sought?"

"No. I found something even better." He sat down and rolled a cigarette. "What brings you here at this hour?"

"In case you have forgotten, I have a client, and I have been down at the city jail talking with him."

"So has Jason Hertz. You know, then, how and why the records were stolen."

"That's why I came here—to tell you."

"That angle's clear enough. What I am interested in most is the time element, and it concerns the movements of that truck driver you were so interested in."

"You found him then."

"Matt did. His name is Charley Kleinhardt."

"And what does he say?"

"Matt forgot to ask him."

"Well I can tell you. In fact I've already told you. It was this truck driver who suggested the time. West's watch, I later learned, was at the jewelers being repaired. So he couldn't have known the hour. Nor could he see the clock above the loading platform from his desk. The driver mentioned that it was about ten o'clock and West took his word for it. In fact he almost forgot the incident."

"I merely wanted to be certain of my facts," said Crole. He removed a sheet of paper from his memorandum book and wrote something on it. "Here," he said, "is the address of Magda Lane. I want her watched."

"Why don't you turn that job over to the police?"

"No, dear. It isn't that easy. She might become frightened and run away. They couldn't stop her, for there's nothing really incriminating against her except what's in my mind."

"And you want me to watch her, and possibly prevent her from leaving the city in case . . ."

"I don't imagine she's quite prepared to leave yet. You're not only to watch her but I want you to call on her. Explain that you're West's attorney, and that Mr. West would like to see and talk with her. She won't be much interested in seeing him. And it doesn't matter at all. It's just that I want you near where you can watch her actions tomorrow morning. But I don't think she'll see you. If you get into a jam and need help, phone Landsdale 331 and ask for Mr. Courtney."

"And who is Mr. Courtney?"

"Courtney," said Crole with quiet emphasis, "is Chief of Naval Intelligence in this area. And I am quite certain that Magda Lane is a person he has been trying to trace with a notable lack of success."

After Esther Manning had left, the private detective dozed in his chair unable to summon the energy to undress.

CHAPTER 19

ALL night long it rained, heavily in the city environs, and with torrential volume in foothills and mountain areas. If the sun shone this Friday morning, the citizens of Los Angeles were not aware of it. They only knew that traffic was snarled, street cars were jammed, schedules disrupted, that sewer mains and gutters were choked with rubble and mud that made street crossing a sorry adventure.

These outward manifestations of nature on a rampage were of scant concern to Simon Crole as he sat on the edge of the davenport where he had fallen to sleep in the early morning hours.

Head cupped in the palms of his hands he peered at the telephone. Its insistent clamor had dragged him forcibly from a deep abyss of sleep.

Languidly he reached for the instrument, sighed and muttered a feeble hello into the receiver.

"Boss," said a voice. "This is Matt."

"Ummm!" grunted Crole. "So what?"

"Listen, I got something on the ball this time. I picked it up in a telephone booth last night, but I couldn't tell you before on account of having to keep my eyes on Russek. He went home and to sleep. Still sleeping, too. Me, I stayed out in the rain and chewed my fingernails."

"You woke me out of a sound sleep, Matt. I'm cross and irritable. If your news can wait . . ."

"Nope, boss. It can't wait. It's hot. Russek called up Jason Hertz last night at San Pedro. Listen. A freighter, *Ramesis*, is twelve miles out from the entrance to the harbor. Two big launches have been chartered to run special freight out to it. Some of the freight is in the warehouse at Pedro. The rest is at the Terminal where I've been laboring. Kleinhardt is to take it out in his trailer tomorrow morning. The launches are to shove off from the pier around twelve o'clock."

Crole became suddenly wide awake. "That's the best report you've ever made, Matt. It's just about perfect. Don't stay with Russek any more. Get over to the Terminal and ride in the cab with Charley Kleinhardt if it's humanly possible. If you can't make it, phone me, and we'll try something else."

Hardly had he cut the connection when the operator put through a second call. It was from Esther. She complained with just reasonableness of the cold cab, of steam on the inside of the windows, and rain on the outside which made it almost impossible to see. Miss Lane had politely but firmly refused to grant an interview. And that was that.

"Don't get discouraged," he told her. "Think of Simon. The office is going to be overflowing with police officers when I get down there this morning. I can feel it in my bones. Call me later. If I haven't erred in my timing, my telephone line will no longer be tapped. 'Bye."

Before going up the elevator to his office, he made a discreet telephone call. His secretary's report confirmed his hunch regarding police officers. He left the phone booth and went to a swank restaurant. Here he had a heart-to-heart talk with the head waiter.

Having planned his breakfast, he went directly to his office.

The place was as he expected it would be—only more so. Steam from all these people's soaking garments fogged the windows. And individual pools of water had formed miniature lakes wherever his callers sat or stood.

Smiling placidly, the private detective removed coat and hat, hung them carefully in their proper places and took stock of the situation. Through the open door to his private office he saw Chief O'Connor, Captain Jorgens, and District Attorney Minifie.

Standing next to the fogged windows were Detectives Gonzales and Chambers, hands in their pockets, eyes roving furtively. Next to the Blue Squad detectives stood Officer Merkle in a natty uniform. He was smoking a cigarette with short, jerky puffs.

In the reception room were Ursula Gault and Inspector Fletcher. Some of the bleakness had vanished from Miss Gault's eyes and mouth. And there was the faintest tinge of color in her gaunt cheeks.

Crole turned to his old friend the Inspector. "What is it, Ira?"

"Nothing particular. I was wondering how you were getting along. I haven't seen you since Wednesday night." His thumb stabbed towards the private office. "What is this — a pinch?"

"Who knows, Ira. I don't. Perhaps you'd better remain. Bring in a chair for yourself and Miss Gault. It's a little early for a session of this kind, but I guess I'll have to face it."

While the Inspector took chairs, himself and Miss Gault into the crowded private office, Crole leaned down and spoke to his secretary: "Is there anything I ought to know before the inquisition starts?"

"Nothing, boss, except that I'm scared. Are you in a jam?" Her eyes were troubled.

"No, precious. My hands and soul are spotless. Keep close to the switchboard. I'm expecting calls from Matt and Esther—important calls. Also, watch the door. It's about time for my breakfast to arrive." He patted her hand, straightened, searched for the most benign of smiles, found it and wore it on his face as he entered entered the crowded office.

"Ah, gentlemen," he beamed, "I hope you will pardon my delayed entrance, but there were certain minor details which had to be attended to." He looked around casually at different faces. "With so many here to greet me, I hardly know where to begin. Perhaps you have already elected a spokesman, and . . ."

Chief O'Connor's fist crashed to the desk top. "We don't need any spokesman, Crole. What I have to say can be said in a few words. It concerns the records stolen from Gene Scanlon's office on the night he was murdered. You had them in your possession. Where are they now?"

"A fair question," said Crole, tossing somebody's overcoat out of his chair, "deserves a like answer. Unfortunately, I am not in a position to give one. Only Gonzales and Chambers can do that."

Detective Gonzales stepped forward. "So you think me and Chambers got 'em, eh? How you gonna prove it?"

Crole said to Captain Jorgens: "Were the records delivered to Headquarters?"

Jorgens scowled. "No."

Chief O'Connor swung on the Blue Squad detectives. "How about it. Did you, or didn't you take them? And don't lie, or try to cover up."

"The private dick is crazy," said Chambers, wiping the back of a hand across his lips.

"It might help your memory," said Crole, "to know that I followed your car. You and Gonzales drove straight to the Red Star garage on Alameda street. At this point you either turned the boxes over to someone else, or they were burned on the premises. An examination of the garage's incinerator might help, Captain Jorgens."

The Captain seized the phone, put through a call and returned to his chair. As he did so there was some confusion at the corridor door as three waiters with trays came into the reception room.

"What the devil's this nonsense?" complained the District Attorney, speaking for the first time.

"My breakfast, Mr. District Attorney. I have to eat just like any other human being. Ah, gentlemen," to the waiters. "Place the trays on my desk. Fine. Pardon the cursory examination. Chops, eggs, griddle cakes, toast, hot rolls . . . good. Excellent service. And the coffee. Ummmm. Just the right temperature. Extend to the Chef my best wishes."

From the first tray he removed a small linen cloth which he spread carefully before him on the desk. With even more care he tucked a napkin beneath his chin.

"Don't mind me, gentlemen," he told them peering expectantly beneath silver-lidded platters. "Eating with so many people around will be somewhat of a trial, but I assure you that I will not falter. Ah! The chops. I'll start in with the chops, gentlemen. You can start from whatever angle you wish."

He neatly separated the meat from the bone, tucked the meat into his mouth and nodded in the direction of the District Attorney. "Slightly underdone," he said, "but not enough to destroy the flavor." He ate two more chops with evident relish.

"Who killed Gene Scanlon?" shouted Chief O'Connor.

"Eh?" The silver lid above the griddle cakes clattered noisily. "It isn't necessary to bellow, Chief. How do I know who killed Gene Scanlon. I was in the audience with the rest of you when the shooting occurred." He spread butter, syrup and sour cream over his griddle cakes, and cut them into triangular wedges. "As I just remarked, I was in the audience—at a table rather—and a guest of a New York Police officer. He'll vouch for that fact."

"Damn well I'll vouch for the fact," rumbled Inspector Fletcher, "and anything else you get off your chest."

Crole speared a luscious wedge and regarded it longingly. "If the question is in order, I'd like to know why Gene Scanlon happened to be at the banquet."

"I found out," said Captain Jorgens, "that he was invited by a man high in the city councils—a respected and high-placed member of the Civil Service Commission. He was invited by Mr. Alvin Russek. And that's that."

Crole ate the wedge of griddle cakes and said between moments of reflective chewing: "Alvin is not here. Why? He *should* be. This hearing is extremely important. He asked Gene Scanlon to be at the meeting for one reason only—he wanted Gene killed in such an unusual setting that everyone who feared Scanlon would have a perfect alibi."

"Which lets everyone in this room out," said Gonzales, "except the dame."

"When you have occasion to refer to Miss Gault again," said Inspector Fletcher, ominously, "skip the dame part, or I'll knock your goddam head off."

Ursula Gault moved closer to the Inspector. And there was a revealing, conscious pride in the movement.

"Getting back to the murder of Scanlon," Crole resumed as the last wedge of griddle cakes followed the same fate as the chops, "there is a little history involved. It concerns two groups of people."

"Get on with it," snapped Chief O'Connor. "We haven't got all day to hang around this office."

"Gonzales, Chambers, Merkle and others," Crole continued, "represented one group within the police department. Their activities were confined to shaking down the drivers of trucks for various infractions of the traffic code. Instead of taking their victims to court, they took the money of the drivers instead. Gordon West of the Trans-Pacific Freight Lines didn't like the racket. He protested to the police and got nowhere. The drivers were afraid to back him up. So he went to Gene Scanlon, hired him to collect evidence, and waited with commendable patience for Scanlon to do something."

Crole stopped to unroll the napkin in which were concealed hot rolls. Liberally spreading them with butter seemed a delightful task. But the pouring of the first cup of coffee from a huge urn was a rite that demanded his utmost concentration. He accomplished it to his complete satisfaction and resumed.

"Scanlon collected plenty, but was wary about turning the evidence over to West. He may have been paid by the group I mentioned not to turn the evidence over to West. That, of course, will have to be proven. West, suspecting the man of double-crossing him, came to my office. His manner of approaching me did not arouse my interest. So I declined to have anything to do in the matter."

He stopped for a moment to savor his coffee. It was good. "That same night Scanlon was killed. I have in my possession a picture of the murderer."

Between bites on the hot roll and sipping of coffee he told in detail how he had obtained the picture.

O'Connor shook his head as he and Jorgens bent over the picture taken by the Candid Camera operator. "Too indistinct to be used as evidence."

"Quite right," agreed Crole, pouring himself more coffee. "Keep the picture, Chief. It's more important than you think."

"About this second group," said the District Attorney. "Suppose you explain. . . ."

"Of course, of course, Mr. District Attorney, but I haven't finished with the first group yet." He turned and said abruptly to Officer Merkle. "Merkle, the man you claimed to have shot in self-defense, was not a truck driver. He was a member of Naval Intelligence. He was also working for Scanlon. If you won't talk to your superiors, there are men in this city who will make you talk."

Merkle's face whitened. "I ain't saying a word."

"You haven't as yet, Merkle. But you're going to. You're going to explain exactly how Ed Corea met his death. If you don't, you're going to go on trial in a Federal Court. Your superiors have been lenient with you because you are a member of the force. But these men in Naval Intelligence won't be lenient at all. You didn't kill

Corea as you said you did. That bullet hole through your cap won't help your story. Rather, it will disprove it. Perhaps you're thinking that Alvin Russek will be able to crush all these proceedings. That time is past. He won't be able to do a thing for you. Alvin Russek, himself, is on the suspect list of Naval Intelligence. Are you ready to come clean and talk?"

Merkle rubbed the palm of a hand across his forehead. "What do you want to know?"

"Who shot Ed Corea, then traded guns with you?"

"Honest," said Merkle, leaning against the wall. "I can't tell you. I don't know. He was a man close to Russek. Drove a black sedan. He shot Corea. I didn't like the rough stuff, but I had to take it. This man made me. Russek's got something on me, on Gonzales, on . . ."

"Shut up!" snapped Gonzales.

"That's enough out of you, Gonzales," growled Chief O'Connor.

"The guy's crazy," insisted the accused detective.

"I'm not crazy," insisted Merkle. "I'm scared. And I'm damn sick of being made a rat out of just because I bought the answers to my Civil Service examination from an agent of Alvin Russek. If there's anything rotten with the police force, Al Russek's to blame. He's got something on most of us."

"Would you know this agent if you saw him again?" asked O'Connor.

Merkle nodded. "I certainly would."

"You'll have your chance, and damn soon."

Crole poured more coffee to drink with his third buttered roll. He did not seem concerned with the proceedings. There was a commotion at the door leading to the corridor. Two squad car officers carrying a cardboard box entered. One of them, Sergeant Breen, saluted Captain Jorgens. "There was nothing to be found in the garage, Captain, so we emptied the ashes from the incinerator into this cardboard container and brought it along for examination."

Jorgens eyed the ashes and twisted metal with doubtful eye. He poked at the blackened material with the end of a pencil. "Hopeless," he said. "Most of the charred fragments of paper have been reduced to small flakes. And I don't think. . . ."

"Miss Gault," Crole interrupted, wiping his lips with a clean napkin. "I'm sure you won't mind soiling your hands. Will you examine the residue of what might once have been the property of your former employee, and see if you can make an identification of any parts of it?"

Ursula Gault crossed the room, knelt beside the box and pawed through it. On the floor she laid a flat piece of metal with three snap-rings attached. "Mr. Scanlon's ledger, or what's left of it. I know it well, for it was my job to take care of the accounts. Its loss won't bankrupt the heirs to the estate for I have made a duplicate from memory."

Chief O'Connor regarded her shrewdly. "You got that kind of a mind?"

"I've a perfect memory," she told him, dragging out a long, metal rod. "This came from the card filing system. I wouldn't be able to tell you anything about the cards because Mr. Scanlon always kept them in his own desk. This twisted box was used for petty cash. It was always crooked, and I could never shut it tightly. The rest of the rubbish must have come from the garage. I don't remember ever seeing it before."

"Thank you, Miss Gault," bowed Crole. He turned and faced the Blue Squad detectives. "Still denying you took these records from my office?"

"Bunk!" scoffed Gonzales, "and you know it. You framed us with the help of this wall-eyed dame. . . ."

That was as far as he got. In three strides Ira Fletcher was across the room. Gonzales whirled—but too late. The Inspector's fist knocked him sprawling to the floor. He rolled over and drew a gun from his shoulder holster. The Inspector kicked it out of his hand. Detective Chambers covered the Inspector with blue-nosed .45 Colt. "Quit it," he ordered. He faced the rest of the group as Gonzales lurched to his feet.

"We're leaving," he said. "We aren't hanging around to be framed by a private dick."

"That's right," added Gonzales. "When the hearing comes up, pass the word along, and we'll come forward. And if any man tries to stop me, it's just gonna be too bad for him. I'll take care of you later on, Fletcher. Nobody socks me and gets away with it."

"Put down your gun, Gonzales, and I'll sock you again."

The two detectives said nothing, but slowly backed from the office, and out into the corridor.

Inspector Fletcher turned angrily on O'Connor. "You letting them crooked dicks get away with it?"

Chief O'Connor grinned. "Skip it, Inspector. They aren't getting away with anything. Think I came up here without making certain arrangements beforehand?"

"In any event," Crole remarked, "these men are not important right now in solving two murders." From his pocket he removed the letter written by Scanlon to Ed Corea. He handed it to the Chief.

The head of the Police Department read it and passed it on to Captain Jorgens. Then it went to the hands of the District Attorney. Having read it they looked to the private detective for interpretation.

"Questions?" asked Crole.

"If this is Scanlon's original letter to Corea," said O'Connor, "then the one I have is a forgery."

"Correct. And the forgery is mine." He paused as if to recall the contents of the letter. "The Big Shot mentioned, is Alvin Russek. And the one whose initials are down on paper as N. F. E. is the first thief. The Blue Squad detectives were second thieves. Does that suggest anything?"

"Not much," scowled Chief O'Connor.

"If you gentlemen will go now," Crole suggested, "and leave me alone with Captain Jorgens, we'll have this N. F. E. as well as the murderer of Scanlon and Corea in custody before tonight."

"Just like that?" shrugged O'Connor doubtfully.

Crole nodded. "Take it or leave it, Chief. I prefer to work in my own way with the assistance of Captain Jorgens. Any interference at this point will complicate matters."

"I'd suggest," said the District Attorney, rising, "that you let Crole have his way in this instance, Chief O'Connor. So far as I am able to judge, he has the situation well in hand."

"All right," grumbled the Chief. "For today only. If nothing develops by tonight, I'll take things in my own hands, and I won't handle anyone with kid gloves. Come on, Merkle. You're going down to Headquarters and talk."

The three men left the office.

Inspector Fletcher came over to Crole's desk. "Anything I can do to help, Simon?"

"Nothing, Ira, except to take good care of Miss Gault."

"As long as I live, Simon, I'll take good care of that girl."

A moment after the couple had left, the phone rang. Esther Manning's voice flowed over the wires: "Calling from the Sante Fe station. Magda's here in the Waiting Room. I think she's about to skip out of town. I've phoned Lansdale 331. Waiting for someone to come. If no one relieves me, am I to take the same train she does?"

"Don't let the woman out of your sight, my dear. Courtney will be there in a few minutes. And he'll handle the situation as he thinks best. But don't let her out of your sight."

"Who was that?" asked Jorgens, suspiciously.

"Miss Manning, Captain. She's working on the Naval Intelligence angle of this case. It looks like a Federal pinch."

CHAPTER 20

JASON HERTZ took down the receiver of his telephone. "Hello," he spoke into the mouthpiece.

A voice said: "Simon Crole speaking. I'm afraid, Mr. Hertz, that your partner is in deeper trouble than I first suspected. Those records you turned over to my office didn't help. Certain police officers broke in and stole them. Later they burned them. So Scanlon's investigation of the racketeers won't help West at all. I thought I'd better tell you. The police, of course, know that you had these records, and I think they suspect you of being a prime mover in the case. I thought you ought to know this. If you could come down to my office, we might map out some kind of defense. You probably don't know Officer Merkle. At the present time he is talking his head off. Will you come down to my office so we can plan what's best to be done?"

Jason Hertz moistened his lips. "Why, why yes," he said, after a moment of hesitation. "Yes. I'll be glad to help." A frozen smile congealed his face. "How about late afternoon?"

"That will be fine," said the voice of the private detective. "I'll be expecting you, Hertz."

Captain Jorgens took a deep breath. "That call you just made, Simon. Mind repeating the exchange number."

"EDmonston 3939."

"Is that the Trans-Pacific?"

"Look in the telephone directory the same as I had to."

"I can do that, too," announced Jorgens, reaching for the thick book. He thumbed through the names until he reached Trans-Pacific, stared for several moments at the listing, then slammed the book back on the desk. "When in hell did that occur to you?"

"Be more explicit, Captain."

"Explicit my eye. That telephone number. It's listed under Night Freight, EDmonston 3939. Damn it, it's the key to the murder."

"So it is,. Captain."

"I'm thinking of those words Scanlon spoke just before he died. You figured he was saying *Night Freight, Ed*. Well, you were right just like you're always right, damn you. Scanlon was trying to get a telephone number across—the Trans-Pacific's San Pedro Terminal that's listed in the book under Night Freight, EDmonston 3939. Only his voice quit after saying only the first two letters of the Exchange word."

"Exactly, Captain. You're shrewder than I suspected."

"Skip it. Who's at that telephone number?"

"Jason Hertz."

"So it's Hertz, then? And he's coming here to give testimony that will convict him of mur— . . ."

"No," said Crole, shaking his head sadly. "Mr. Hertz is not that stupid. He's a brainy man. He won't be coming to my office. The fact that I planted the idea that Merkle was talking will start him thinking. He'll do a little checking up amongst his confederates. He'll discover that Gonzales and Chambers are in the dog-house. He'll make a decision—and a fast one. In other words, Hertz will leave town.

"And since, Captain, as I have just said, Hertz is no fool, he will not come to my office. He was the original first thief of Scanlon's records. While those records were in his possession, he undoubtedly destroyed everything of an incriminating nature, and turned the useless residue over to me. The boys from the Blue Squad, not yet having learned of what he had done, undertook the same weeding-out process. Evidently there was dynamite in those records."

"Then how are we going to convict?"

"Through Merkle's statements, and the confession of the actual killer."

"If Jason Hertz is as brainy as you think, he won't talk. He won't even be in the city."

"You labor," sighed Crole, "under the erroneous impression that Hertz is the killer. He isn't. He's simply a sharp-edged tool being used by Alvin Russek. And Russek, working with this woman, Magda Lane, is the contact man with foreign agents who are anxious to acquire certain mechanical and aviation secrets belonging to our government."

"So that's where the Naval Intelligence fits into the picture. Then why in hell isn't Magda Lane placed under arrest? Why haven't you told me about Hertz before? Someday these damned dilatory tactics of yours aren't'going to jell, and . . ."

The door to the reception room opened. Into the private office clumped Matt Ridley. He was covered with mud from head to foot.

"Hi, boss," he called out. "H'are yuh, Captain."

Simon Crole looked the least bit cross. "I thought you were going to phone me, Matt. I've been expecting . . ."

"Sorry, boss, but it didn't work out. I've been in an accident. We were taking that freight I told you about to San Pedro. And we were rolling over a concrete bridge when the center span, weakened by flood waters, collapsed completely, and our truck went with it into the river. I ain't kidding you. I thought I was kicked by four mules. I went through that front windshield like nobody's business and into that boiling river that looked like the Mississippi at flood time. But Charley wasn't so lucky. I scrambled out of the water and dragged him with me. He had a broken leg and couldn't walk. He's in the hospital at Costa Hermo."

"And the freight, Matt?"

"I phoned the Chief Dispatcher to send out a wrecking crew. Nothing will happen to that truck right away. It's buried in three feet of water and mud."

But Simon Crole was no longer listening. He was dialing a number—Landsdale 331—on the phone.

"Hello, Lieutenant Grey? Simon Crole. U. S. Highway 101 near Costa Hermo. There's a T.P. truck and trailer in the river. The company wrecking crews are on their way to reclaim it. Get there in a hurry. I've an idea the contents of the trailer will interest you."

He broke the connection and turned to his operator.

"You're finished, Matt. And I might add that you've been magnificent."

"You aren't kidding me, boss?" Ridley knew he was far from being magnificent. Still, he liked to think he was.

"I repeat, Matt, you've been magnificent. Fade now, and come back later in the day. The case is broken and Captain Jorgens and his men are going out to gather up the pieces."

"In that case," nodded Ridley, "I'll be leaving."

He left. And following close behind him staggered a busboy from the restaurant, his arms heaped high with trays.

"Now," resumed Captain Jorgens, "about those pieces to be gathered up, Simon."

"One thing at a time. I've already mentioned the janitor at the *Commodore*. Get him quietly down to Headquarters without anyone

knowing it. Next, Hertz will have to be watched. His first move
will be to come to the city where he can make discreet inquiries.
Undoubtedly, he'll go home first. From that point we can pick up
his trail."

"Want a detective?"

"No, thanks. I want someone who is not too smart, and who is
not known to Mr. Hertz. How about Patrolman Doyle?"

"You're using him quite a lot, aren't you?"

"More than you're aware of. He's a good man, and my secretary's
very sweet on him at the moment, so it works out fine for everybody.
Call Doyle. Have him go to the home of Mr. Hertz." He wrote the
address on the telephone memorandum pad. "If Hertz reveals any
signs of leaving the city, instruct Doyle to place him under arrest."

Captain Jorgens issued terse instructions over the phone. Bang-
ing the instrument back into its cradle he said: "We aren't getting
anywheres, Simon. I want the name of the killer. That's all that's
important right now."

"You won't believe me when I tell you."

"The hell I won't."

"His name is Kleinhardt—Charley Kleinhardt."

"No, Simon." Captain Jorgens shook his head gloomily. "You'll
have to make another guess. Maybe you think I've been sitting
around waiting for you to save my job for me. Now listen. I talked
with West. I also talked with this driver, Kleinhardt. West insists
he was at the Terminal at ten o'clock. And Kleinhardt substantiates
the time, for he was *also* there as West will testify. So was Jason
Hertz. There goes your solution, Simon. Try something else."

Simon Crole smiled complacently. "Has it occurred to you, Captain, that Kleinhardt went into West's office for one reason only—
namely to establish a time alibi for himself just in case he was ever
suspected? If it hasn't, you'd better pause and reflect. West carried
no watch at the time. It was being repaired at the jewelers. It was
Kleinhardt who furnished the time. The Terminal clock wasn't
visible from where West sat at his desk. So he could not know the
hour unless it was suggested to him by someone else."

"Hertz could have told him."

"Hertz wasn't there. He told me so himself. The element of time
hadn't yet entered into his plans. By such mistakes are murderers
trapped. Here, substantially, is what occurred. At nine o'clock
Hertz and West broke into Scanlon's office and secured all the private detective's records. It didn't take long—not more than ten
minutes. At the curb the two men separated. Hertz was to take

the records to his own home, and West had his mind on something else—a meeting with a dear friend, Miss Magda Lane.

"But he decided, and didn't tell Hertz, to go instead to his office to clean up some important contracts, and was there some time before nine-thirty. Since West trusted Hertz implicitly, it never occurred to him that Hertz would destroy the very evidence he, himself, was so anxious to obtain. Hertz did just that and then turned the purged records over to me. But he overlooked one item on a small card. And this proved very damaging. I refer to the telephone memo: *In emergency call T. P. EDmonston 3939.* Here it is," handing the card to the Captain.

"I'll admit Hertz tricked me. I'll also admit that this action of his has weakened the District Attorney's chances of completely purging the Police Department. But it hasn't weakened my case against Charley Kleinhardt. Keep in mind, also, that Kleinhardt was having a day off from work on Wednesday when Corea was shot."

He raised his hand palm outwards as Jorgens began to squirm in his chair. "Wait a minute, Captain, I haven't finished. West then went back to the Terminal following the robbery at Scanlon's office. And while he was there Kleinhardt came in, talked about his three wives, then looked at his watch and made mention of the hour. But his watch must have been very, very fast for he left the Terminal and was at the *Commodore* by a quarter of ten."

He removed the Candid Camera picture from the desk drawer. "See this picture of the murderer and the janitor in the background? Of course you've already seen it, and your comment that the faces were too indistinct to be used as evidence was natural. But—those indistinct figures in the picture are not my reason for showing you this camera shot a second time. Observe, if you will, the cars parked at the curb. One of them, the second from the machine in the foreground, is a dark sedan. Now, if Kleinhardt was in West's office at around ten o'clock, how is it that his car, registered in his name, is parked close to the *Commodore* shortly before a murder was committed? Now, don't take *my* word regarding the time element. Question the janitor."

"Hmmm!" Captain Jorgens regarded the picture with mounting interest. "I think," he said, judiciously, "that you've got something."

"Then I'd suggest that you start gathering up the pieces, and leave the thinking to me. Kleinhardt's in the hospital at Costa Hermo. But there's no telling how long he'll remain there if word reaches him that the net is closing in. You can take full credit for the arrest. And when you're ready, I'll come down to Headquarters."

CHAPTER 21

LONG after Captain Jorgens had left, the phone rang. Crole eyed the instrument uneasily and thrust it against his ear. "Agency of Simon Crole. . . ."

"You're a lout," came a woman's voice over the wire, "a stupid, senseless lout. When you need a woman operator again, call on someone else. I positively refuse to work for you. I've got a law practise of my own that is more important to me than chasing mirages and making a fool out of myself."

Crole's eyebrows moved up. "But Esther, dear. Why all the disenchantment and tears? Did Miss Lane elude you?"

"Idiot," she scolded. "You scheming idiot, where, heaven's name, did you gather the information that was supposed to incriminate Miss Lane, and make a criminal out of her?"

"From my head. Listen. It was a case of perfect reasoning. This happened. That happened. I made my deductions and determined on a course of action. Did I err?"

"Did you err? You made a colossal blunder. Know who Magda Lane is? You don't or you wouldn't have sent me out in the cold and wet to watch her apartment. Well, my all-wise friend, Magda Lane was working with Mr. Courtney of Naval Intelligence. And my muddling into her affairs came to an end at the Santa Fe station when Courtney appeared on the scene. That's what happened. Now, if you—but what's the use. . . ."

"Don't hang up," said Crole, mildly. "Is Courtney still with you at the station? Good. Let me talk with him."

A moment later: "Courtney? I'll explain later about the misunderstanding. I discovered that Magda Lane was putting on an act, that she was not blind. It doesn't matter how I found this out. The important thing is to make your moves fast."

"That's exactly what I'm doing. But your woman operator's phone call bringing me to the Santa Fe hasn't helped. Miss Lane was to have met Russek here, and if Russek appeared and observed all of us together, I'm afraid he would have quietly withdrawn."

"Don't figure on Russek being anywhere near the Santa Fe station. Right now he's over at the pier warehouse of the Trans-Pacific in San Pedro waiting for a load of hot freight to arrive. It

121

will never get there. The truck and trailer crashed through a weakened bridge. I sent Lieutenant Grey to cover it and place it under guard pending an examination.

"Now listen a little longer. Russek's charted two big, fast launches. And he plans to run everything stolen from the trucks of the Trans-Pacific out to a freighter, *Ramesis*, some twelve miles out of the harbor. I intended to call you about this before, but there has been an inquisition going on in my office."

"It's eleven o'clock," said Courtney. "Have you any idea when Russek's launches are heading out to sea?"

"Around noon, my informant told me. You'll have to hurry to get there before. . . ."

"Don't worry. I'll telephone on ahead and the warehouse will be placed under immediate observation. Not even a rowboat will be able to get through the outer harbor. See you later."

"Right," said Crole, breaking off the connection.

He removed a handkerchief from his breast pocket and wiped his forehead. Mentally he reviewed the case for loose threads of investigation. There didn't seem to be any.

He relaxed in his chair. The office became intensely quiet. Deftly he rolled a cigarette, lighted it and inhaled with pleasureable content. A half hour passed. By this time, he reasoned, Kleinhardt had been placed under arrest. A second half hour followed the first. Courtney must now be in San Pedro. His phone rang.

The voice of Charlotte West was like the ringing of a happy bell in the private detective's ears. "Gordon just got home," she said, "and I'm grateful. More grateful than I can tell you over the phone. Captain Jorgens told him that all the credit should go to the right man—namely, Simon Crole."

It was on Crole's mind to hint delicately about payment for services. But he had disciplined himself against any such gross betrayal of his baser instincts. "Thank you," he said, simply. "Now I have a pleasant surprise for you. Your husband need never know I told you. It will remain a secret between the two of us. Miss Lane is not his mistress, and probably never was. She is connected with an organization I am not at liberty to disclose. And her interest in him has been purely professional. You can forget about this woman. She passes out of the picture at this point."

"I wouldn't be human not to feel happy, Mr. Crole. Will you do me a special favor and accept one from me?"

"It depends. I'll do my best."

"Come to my home tonight — to dinner. Grandpaw Horschel

keeps asking about you. So does Peter. I think you've charmed the boy. He talks of nothing else but the man who makes coins disappear. Please come."

"I'll accept the invitation with a great deal of pleasure, Mrs. West. Until tonight then at . . ."

"At eight."

"Fine. I'll see you and your family then at that time."

At two o'clock Captain Jorgen's exultant voice crackled from the telephone receiver: "Kleinhardt's been placed under arrest. We brought him to Headquarters in an ambulance. There was't any fight left in him. The janitor from the *Commodore* made a positive identification. So did Officer Merkle. Under cross-questioning Kleinhardt was tripped into a number of false statements. Finally he broke down and signed a complete confession which involved nearly thirty men on and off the force, among them Russek and Jason Hertz. We've also got Hertz at Headquarters. Doyle brought him in just as the man was getting ready to leave the city by plane. Russek, however, is still loose along with Gonzales and Chambers."

"Don't lose any sleep about Russek, Captain. Naval Intelligence is not sleeping. I have a notion that he's been under federal arrest for the past two hours. I pulled all the strings at the same time. My task is ended."

"Okay. Come down in the morning then."

Simon Crole pushed the telephone away as though it had become suddenly distasteful. The door to the reception room was opening. Courtney, Esther and the beautiful Magda Lane were coming through the doorway.

He rose gallantly, walked around his desk and helped his visitors into chairs. To Esther he said: "My humble apologies, Esther, dear. Never have I been so utterly desolated."

Esther said drily: "Lout!"

Crole turned to Courtney. "Was my information worth while?"

The Naval Intelligence officer nodded. "It was worth exactly ten thousand dollars. The Navy, itself, would probably scoff at such an amount. But we of the Intelligence have a special fund — one that is never audited. You will be paid this sum, Mr. Crole, not for services to the nation, but for absolute forgetfulness. I trust the point is clear to you."

"It isn't. Have you arrested Alvin Russek?"

"Yes."

"Think you can convict him?"

"We've been watching him for weeks without success. Miss Lane was close to his secret connections when you intervened. "

"He'll be indicted with others for conspiracy, felony, and murder," said Crole. "And I expect to be called in to testify. Will you please explain how I am to attain absolute forgetfulness?"

"His name will never be brought up, Crole. Understand? He will be forgotten, apparently. City officers will be dismissed from the force. Those guilty of any crimes will be punished. There will be no general shake-up on the police force. Even the press will play down the news. I hope you understand that secrecy is our only defense."

"Only vaguely."

"Will you accept the sum offered you?"

"You place me and my agency in a vulnerable position, Courtney."

"You placed yourself there when you reasoned that Edward Corea was murdered, and not accidentally killed."

"Basing your premise on that angle alters the situation. I accept your offer, Courtney."

"Very good. A check will be delivered to your office this afternoon. By the way, Miss Lane would like a few words with you."

Crole nodded and turned to Magda Lane. There was no blank, glassy look in her eyes now. They were sparkling and clear, and of an altogether different color. Where once they had a pale, washed-out blue about them, they were now a deep violet. Those violet eyes looked mystically in his. Her lips parted. She said: "I believe, Simon Crole, that you have something of mine. Something that is a secret I don't care to have known but to few people. Before you return it, will you tell me how you knew?"

"Believe me," he smiled. "Your blindness was the most perfect disguise I have ever seen. I believed in it implicitly until . . ."

"Go on, please."

"Gordon West thought a great deal of you. And it was my impression after talking with him and Jason Hertz, that someone — not you particularly, was obtaining information from West regarding certain shipments of value. I determined to investigate. I went to your apartment and stationed myself on a hill behind the building. Russek was there. When he left, I had my operator follow him. It was this operator who heard Russek give final instructions by telephone to his agents in San Pedro."

"You succeeded where I failed," said Magda. "My charms, evidently, were not so alluring as I had imagined."

"They are more alluring than you think," observed Crole. "However, as I watched your windows following Russek's departure, I observed the lights go on in your bedroom, and I saw you draw the shades. And the thought came to me: Why should a blind woman need lights at night when she lives always in darkness?"

She smiled.

"I waited until I thought you must be asleep, then I broke into your apartment. I looked for something else, and I found this." From his vest pocket he removed a cup-like structure of special lense glass that fits over the eyeball, and under the eyelid. It was a delicate reproduction of a human eye down to the last tiny veins. "You see," he explained, "if this were clear glass, it would be easily recognizable as the new type of optical aid — something that takes the place of ordinary eye glasses. The second my fingers touched it while exploring the top of your dressing table, the secret of your blindness was known to me.

"So it was natural to assume that you were not a friend of Gordon West, my client, but an enemy, a traitor to a man who trusted you. Aside from Esther Manning, whom I am certain has not missed a word of this explanation, and myself, there is no one aware of your quaint idiosyncrasy of wanting to be thought of as blind. And I can promise that this knowledge will never get beyond this office."

She took the delicate, cup-like object from his fingers and moved to a far corner of the room. When she returned and faced him again, she was the Magda Lane whom he had first seen and talked with. Her eyes were again vacant with glassiness.

"Mr. Russek might need me," she explained. "I was supposed to have met him this morning, but . . . Still, there may be some contacts to make — someone he may trust me to talk with, someone who is higher in intrigue than he is."

Crole looked at her as one would some strange symbol of courage. "Then your work is not ended, Miss Lane?"

She smiled and stared at a spot above his head. "The work I do is never ended, Mr. Crole. And that's the lure of it. Life would be dull and drab without the darkness and light I live with. Someday, I hope we'll meet again."

He took her arm and walked with her to the door. Courtney and Esther followed close behind.

"Goodbye," he said. "If you ever get in trouble, and you can't, figuratively, see your way out, will you call on Simon Crole? I feel that I owe you something — an apology that cannot be expressed in mere words."

"I will not forget you," she promised.

The phone was ringing when he returned to his desk. He listened to the hearty voice of Inspector Fletcher. It was also boisterous and happy. There was a quality in it Crole had never heard before. He put down the instrument after a while and went to his secretary's desk.

"I heard," said Etta.

"They're eloping," marvelled Crole. "Imagine that! Why should anyone elope these days. And they're taking Miss Ursula's invalid sister with them to New York."

His lips pursed. "Make out a check," he told her, "payable to Mrs. Ira Fletcher — one thousand dollars. That ought to buy them some wedding presents, hadn't it?"

Etta gasped. "Good Lord, it'll buy a house with a picket fence around it. Have you lost your wits, boss?"

"Precious, I have lost nothing but the ability to judge human beings. I made two errors in this case and they're going to plague me to no end. "Where's Esther?"

"She left with Courtney and Miss Lane." She looked at him sharply. "Didn't you see her leave?"

"No. I was bewitched by violet eyes I could not see."

Utter confusion and indescribable clamor beat against the ears of Simon Crole as he entered the West home. From behind a chair Peter West sprayed him with imaginary bullets. Grandpaw Horschel, striding from a spot near the fireplace, tipped over brass firetongs and shovel.

"Evening!" he yelled. "By jeepers, it's good to see you again, Mr. Coal. Peter, turn off that rattle in your throat. A fellow can't hear himself talk. Take off your coat, neighbor. Sharley's fixing up a little nip."

Charlotte West came in and held out both hands.

Crole took them in his own. "Am I late?"

"It wouldn't matter if you were — not in *this* house."

"Where's Gordon?"

"Upstairs. He wanted me to send you up the moment you came — before the family gathered for dinner." She pulled her hands free from his and took a sealed envelope from the fireplace mantel. "I have some money in my own right, Simon Crole, and I am giving you this out of a gratitude I can't express. . . ."

"Please, no," he protested, wondering as he did so how much the envelope contained.

"It's a woman's prerogative to change her mind or bestow a gift."

"I swear," beamed Crole, "you shall not be deprived of your womanly prerogative. I shall accept your gift."

"Will you do that trick again, Mister?" asked Peter, following the private detective to the foot of the stairs. "You know the one where you put the coin in my hand. . . ."

"Sure, Pete," he beamed on the lad. "That one and a number of others. But not until after supper."

"Okay," smiled the boy.

Surreptitiously, on ascending the stairs to the rooms above where Gordon West awaited him, Simon Crole unsealed the envelope. In it was a check for five thousand dollars. Astonishment pushed his lips open. "This gets better all the time," he told himself.

Gordon West was a business man. And as such he dealt with the private detective. "How much?" he asked, bruskly.

"In cases of this type," Crole explained, "I never render statements. There is no standard by which I can fix charges. Either you're satisfied, or you aren't. The matter is a purely personal arrangement. The emolument is for you to decide."

"Five thousand to your lawyer friend, Miss Manning. Ten thousand to you. You'll be underpaid for your actual services to me. You've probably saved my life. Satisfied?"

"I'm not a man to quibble," said Crole. "Make out your checks."

Had there been a clock in the steeple of a nearby church, it would have been tolling the hour of midnight when Simon Crole walked unsteadily, but jauntily from the home of the Wests.

"The lines are fallen unto me in pleasant places," he thought, quoting an obscure passage of scripture. "Yea," he continued, smiling benignly as he peered down the street for a night-cruising taxi, "I have a goodly heritage."

THE END